PARKERSBURG & WOOD COUNTY PUBLIC LIBRARY

5091 000307920 8

P9-ELX-128

Withdrawn

Parkersburg & Wood County Public Library
3100 Emerson Ave. Parkersburg, WV 26104
304/420-4587
BRANCHES

South   304/428-7041
Waverly   304/464-5668
Williamstown   304/375-6052

Withdrawn

no laughter here

no laughter here

Rita Williams-Garcia

HarperCollins*Publishers*
Amistad

Amistad is an imprint of HarperCollins Publishers Inc.

No Laughter Here
Copyright © 2004 by Rita Williams-Garcia
All rights reserved. No part of this book may be used or
reproduced in any manner whatsoever without written permission except in the case of brief quotations embodied in
critical articles and reviews. Printed in the United States of
America. For information address HarperCollins Children's
Books, a division of HarperCollins Publishers, 1350 Avenue
of the Americas, New York, NY 10019.
www.harperchildrens.com

Library of Congress Cataloging-in-Publication Data
Williams-Garcia, Rita.
    No laughter here / by Rita Williams-Garcia.
    p. cm.
Summary: In Queens, New York, ten-year-old Akilah is
determined to find out why her closest friend, Victoria,
is silent and withdrawn after returning from a trip to
her homeland, Nigeria.
    ISBN 0-688-16247-9—ISBN 0-688-16248-7 (lib. bdg.)
[1. Friendship—Fiction. 2. Schools—Fiction. 3. Coming
of age—Fiction. 4. Female circumcision—Fiction.
5. Nigerian Americans—Fiction. 6. African Americans—
Fiction. 7. Queens (New York, N.Y.)—Fiction.] I. Title.
    PZ7.W6713No 2004
[Fic]—dc21
                                            2003009331

Typography by Sasha Illingworth
1 2 3 4 5 6 7 8 9 10
❖
First Edition

For Stephanie Elaine and Asha Imani,
who can laugh, laugh, laugh.
And for girls who cannot.

no laughter here

Girl Warrior Rising

Did you ever cross your fingers and play that game in your head: If the last Life Saver in the roll is pineapple, then the letter will come this week. If the phone rings only twice before Dad yells, "I got it!," then the letter will come this week. If I can count to ten at my normal counting speed before a floating dandelion hits the ground, then it's for certain: Victoria's letter will definitely come this week.

Ever play that game and the last Life Saver is pineapple, Dad yells for the phone in time, and the dandelion is still crisscrossing above the hydrangeas on the count of twelve, and still no letter from Nigeria?

For two days straight I watched the mailman push his cart by our house only to leave a few Dear Occupant envelopes and a letter from our state assemblywoman.

Today, however, I was ready for him. Instead of watching from my bedroom window, I was stationed downstairs behind the living-room curtains. He was one of those new guys who was filling in while our regular carrier was on vacation. When I got through with him, he'd know that I was expecting an important letter and that his duty was to be on the lookout for anything from Nigeria. Victoria's stamps didn't fall off on their own, I'd explain. Some stamp collector was dazzled by the mighty Chief Obafemi Awolowo or the baobab tree smack in the corner of Victoria's letter and took those stamps for his private collection. I had to remind the mailman that even if the stamps had been taken off—and chances are they had—it was his duty to deliver Victoria's letter through rain, sleet, and from across the Atlantic Ocean.

So when the mailman pushed the cable bill and a leaflet from our councilman through the mail slot, I swung open the front door before he could get away. Dad says I have Girl Warrior rising, meaning I leap into action like a super-shero when action is needed.

"Mr. Mailman," I called after him. "Can you check your bag to see if there are any letters from Nigeria, postage due?"

I didn't even get a chance to tell him to be on the look-out for Victoria's letter and to deliver it even if Chief Obafemi Awolowo had fallen off the corner. Mom snatched me back into the house. Not with her hands. She didn't believe in yanking or spanking. But with her voice.

"Akilah Hunter!"

Girl Warrior fell to earth with a thud. I closed the door quicker than I had opened it.

"You know better than to talk to strangers."

I came inside and sat down on the sofa to sulk. I

couldn't see what the big deal was. After all, during the school year I walk to school and back with a key around my neck, advertising to anyone that I'm a latchkey kid. I ride my bike all over town and no one ever messes with me.

Mom should have let the mailman answer, because now my mind took off into the wild blue yonder as she scolded me.

Victoria's letter had fallen off the mail barge and was floating up the White Nile. It had survived hippos and crocodiles only to drown in Khartoum, where the White Nile meets the Blue Nile. I could see the envelope sinking, sinking . . . but I snapped out of it because Victoria wasn't in Sudan.

"I should have enrolled you in that math and science camp up at York College instead of keeping you home . . . ."

That thought sent me back on the trail of Victoria's letter. Back across the Atlantic Ocean to the African continent.

I saw a rickety truck climbing the mountains of Kenya on bald tires. Mailbags bounced as the truck made its way up the rocky dirt road. A mailbag jostled open. A trail of letters dotted the road like Hansel and Gretel's bread crumbs.

"I thought spending more time together would be a good opportunity . . ."

But Victoria wasn't in Kenya or in Egypt. She wasn't in the Congo, or in Madagascar or Botswana. Victoria was in Nigeria, visiting her grandmother. She and her family had been in Nigeria since June twenty-third, the day I marked on my calendar as the start of Victoria's great journey. It was now August. Two months and only two letters.

Mom was still talking. "Clearly, you need more activities."

I went over our plan to stay in touch, which was, first she'd write, then I'd write, then she'd write, and I'd write, until she returned to Queens. The plan was going well. She wrote. Then I wrote. Then she wrote. Then I wrote. Then two weeks passed since my last letter from Victoria. Then three weeks. I wrote again, addressing the envelope in my clearest handwriting, to make sure it would be delivered, but it was no use. Her letters stopped coming. No more loopty-loo *L*s and jolly *P* stems. No fat-dotted *I*s and *J*s.

I went over everything in my mind, like a rice inspector sifting through barrels of rice. Was it something I wrote in my last letter? I told her a joke I got off the Internet. I asked about the special dinner in her honor—I mean, that's all I heard about before the Ojikes left for Africa: "There will be a special dinner to celebrate my coming-of-age." That was what Mrs. Ojike told Victoria and that was what Victoria told me, over and over.

I admit, I felt jealous and left out. After all, there was something important going on in Victoria's life, and I wasn't a part of it. I was jealous, but I didn't act like a brat. I even asked her about her dress—was it an American dress or an African dress, like her mother always wore. Of course, I asked about Nelson and how he looked. Then I wrote to her about soccer camp and how that stupid Juwan Spenser used every chance he got to kick the ball at me, not to me. But I got him back, and I wrote in detail about that in my last letter.

None of those things would have been enough to make Victoria stop writing to me. Besides, I'd said much worse things to her face and we were still friends, so I knew it wasn't my letter.

I tried to recall everything she said before she left for Nigeria, but nothing strange came to mind. Then I panicked. What if the Ojikes weren't coming back to Queens, and Victoria figured it was pointless being friends if we didn't live in the same country? After all, they left Africa to live in England when she was born, then moved to Queens two years ago. If the Ojikes could hop from country to country so easily, it was only a matter of time before they left Queens for good, wasn't it?

I needed my questions answered. After lunch I got on my bike and rode three blocks up to the Ojikes' rented house to look through their window. All of the furniture was still there, although I realized that could be rented as well. But then I saw Mrs. Ojike's *kente* cloth hanging on the wall. *Kente* cloth is woven on a loom with different-colored threads. My mother admired that cloth so much that Mrs. Ojike took it down to give to her. Then Mom got all embarrassed and wouldn't take it, but I knew she wanted it.

"They're not home."

I turned around. It was Miss Lady from across the street. Her real name is Miss Dorothy Boothe, but you know how you pick a name for someone when you're little and it just sticks? Miss Lady was my sitter when I was little, which I don't understand, because Miss Lady doesn't like kids. She never comes to the door on Halloween. She just lets her dog, Gigi, bark at us.

"I know," I said, still looking inside.

"You shouldn't be playing in their yard." Her voice was nearer. She had crossed the street.

"I'm not playing," I said, not really meaning to back talk, but that's just how it came out. "I just want to see—"

"See what? There's nothing to see."

"If they're coming back."

"You can't see that from there. Now . . . " She was telling me to leave before she called my mama.

Girl Warrior pulled back from the window and rode away. I was already in enough trouble with my mother for talking to strangers.

Backyard Tea Talks

Summer days were extra long. Not because of
daylight savings time, but because Victoria was not a part
of them. All I had to look forward to was soccer at the Y
and finishing a math workbook. Mom never brought
home a fun workbook with creative writing exercises.
*Imagine you are on an island. . . . Imagine you are leading
a wilderness expedition. . . . Imagine you made the discovery of the century. . . .*

About my need to stretch my imagination, Mom
would say, "There's a notebook on your desk. Write."
Then she'd take my math workbook and check it.
Sometimes I got a science workbook to break the monot-
ony. This summer I started with fourth-grade math for
review, then I did fifth-grade workbooks to be on top of
things.

I snuck a peek at the sixth-grade workbook Mom had
waiting for me, just to see what the future looked like.
Instead of going chapter by chapter, I flipped to the
advanced section in the back and found algebra. Unh,
unh, unh. All those years of doing real operations with

real numbers only to have it all thrown out the window for some *AB*s and *XY*s. It just doesn't seem right. Like pushing the world's most humongous boulder up a hill because you have nothing better to do.

I've never seen the cashier count back X change. None of Mom's recipe cards say to measure $2X$ cups of flour, nor do dress patterns call for sewing along a $5/AB$-inch seam.

I looked at the equations and shook my head. Letters mixed with numbers. Unh, unh, unh. There are some things I'm not ready to understand.

This was the boringest summer ever. I banged my legs along the edge of the lawn chair and chanted, "Boring, boring, boring, boring, boring, boring, boring." I sounded like a rusty, broken spring. *Boing. Boing. Boing.*

Mom set down a tray with tuna sandwiches cut in quarters next to our lounge chairs and went back inside for the iced tea. She was keeping me from the front yard, which was where I sat and waited for the mailman or for the Ojikes to return from Africa. Mom said, "What's the sense in having a backyard patio if you just stare at it all winter?"

Sometimes we sit in the backyard and paint each other's nails, recline like movie stars, and sip iced tea.

Both of our chairs were fixed in the upright position, so we weren't doing manicures today. When Mom brought out the raspberry tea and sat down, I stopped saying "Boring, boring" and crossed my legs.

She said in her lazy voice, "You know, girl . . . "

I answered, equally lazy, "What, girl?"

This is how we begin our talks. You don't think my mother would let me call her "girl" in the front yard out in public? Calling each other "girl" is strictly for the backyard. We started when I was five and had Kool-Aid tea parties with animal crackers out on the patio. Now we sip on real herbal tea and talk about anything we want.

Once I untangled myself from missing Victoria, I started feeling how nice it was back here, even with a few flies buzzing around. I remembered how Mom came home from work a mess just before the last day of school, trembling and crying. She said she couldn't believe someone could do *that* to their own daughter. I asked what, but neither she nor Dad answered. They just shooed me up to my room. Anyway, she took a leave from her job at Child Welfare and hasn't been back since.

"Ahhhh." I sipped my raspberry tea with extra sugar. At this moment I loved being an only and having my mother to myself. We wouldn't be enjoying any backyard tea talks if I had brothers and sisters every which where like my cousin Pearlina has. Pearlina is in the middle of nine brothers and sisters. Auntie Cass only has time to tell my cousins what they better do and not do. Pearlina always says I am so lucky.

Mom set her glass down. She said, "It's time we had this talk."

Her tone sent me racing to think of things I had forgotten to do or had done wrong. I had already been properly scolded for talking to the mailman, so I knew that was over. My room is always neat. Sort of. I couldn't think of anything we had to talk about.

"We're early bloomers," she began.

I wiped the huh-what? off my face and tried to follow what she was saying. I consider myself lightning quick, but I was looking stupid until she said, "You're already starting your changes. You're so much like I was. I bloomed early."

I knew it was happening, but I didn't want to bloom. Have you even seen a rose in full bloom? All the petals open as wide as they can and then they fall off. I will not bloom. I will not bloom. If I bloom, someone will try to pick me. Yank me from my stem and—

"Akilah. Focus. Listen to me."

I didn't want to focus. I wanted to take off on one of my trips into the wild blue yonder. Unfortunately Mom knew this and kept my feet on the ground.

"Those little stomachaches you're getting are your body's way of preparing for your menstrual cycle. I'm telling you about it now so you won't panic when your first period comes."

"Why do I have to think about that now?" I said. "I still have two years to be a girl."

"Two years to be a girl?" My mother looked at me like she hadn't heard me correctly, which wasn't possible. She can hear me muttering under my breath in the next room.

"Victoria and I aren't in any rush to get our periods.

We're getting it at twelve like everyone else."

Mom started to laugh. She felt bad for a minute, stopped, and then laughed anyway. "I have news for you," she said, wiping her tears. "This is nothing you can control. You will get it when it comes, and chances are, that will be when you're eleven."

I know a little more about periods than I do about algebra. Debra Wells, this sixth grader, told Victoria and me that girls get their periods and boys get stupid. She said there are fifty kinds of sanitary pads, but just call them Kotex when you need one. Everybody does.

After our talk with Debra Wells, Victoria and I had to check out the mystery of sanitary napkins for ourselves. We snuck into the teachers' bathroom with a quarter and bought a Kotex from the vending machine. We opened the wrapper and dissected the napkin like it was our science project. When we saw that it was just cotton wrapped in cotton, Victoria said, "We should have bought gum with the quarter." She was right. We could have split the gum.

Wish up the Moon

When the sandwiches and raspberry tea were finished, and the talk about periods and blooming was over, Mom said we should go shopping for school shoes. She grabbed her car keys and we went out front to the driveway. I don't know what made me look to the right, but I did and, boy, I must have leaped up in the air fifty feet when I saw the car coming up the street. I couldn't stop jumping and hollering and waving like a maniac.

"Akilah. Akilah."

I heard Mom's voice, the stop-that-right-nowness in her tone, but I kept jumping.

Then the car was right alongside us. Mr. Ojike slowed down as they approached, but he didn't stop. He waved to Mom and me. Not excitedly, but carefully, the way stilt walkers in parades balance and wave. Victoria's brother, Nelson, nodded, which normally would have made me silly, but for once I didn't care about Nelson. I waved and screamed and jumped, but Victoria didn't look up. She didn't turn, move, or do anything. So I stopped jumping and waving.

Their car crawled past us, all slow. It reminded me of the line of black cars that trailed behind us at Grandpa Jack's funeral. Once again I thought of everything I had written to Victoria. Everything and anything that would make her mad at me.

Mom placed her hand on my shoulder. "She's just tired."

I wanted to believe her, but I knew something was wrong. My thoughts must have been sitting out there as big as day. Mom said, "Victoria's crossed over the Atlantic and a few time zones. She must be worn out, baby." One thing: My mother does not baby me. That's Dad's job.

"Can I—"

"No," Mom said firmly. "Let them settle in."

We got into the car and pulled out of the driveway.

"Tomorrow?"

"Tomorrow."

Wish up the moon. Wish up the moon. Tomorrow just wasn't getting here soon enough. Finally a sliver of moon showed itself, but the sky wasn't dark enough for night-time. Stupid summer nights. We'd never have a new day at this rate, and you can't get tomorrow started unless you're done with today.

Once it was dark outside, truly owl-hooting dark, cricket-chirping dark, I made deals to bring up the sun: I'll send over the moon if you hand over the sun. No one was paying me any mind. The sun was just tra-la-laing along, down in New Zealand. Australia. Way, way down under.

Somewhere between wishing down the moon and trading it in for the sun, I fell asleep.

I woke up expecting to see the sun, but it was still dark. Not just-before-the-cock-crows dark, but dark as in the moon wasn't going nowhere, no time soon. In fact, according to my clock, I had been asleep for only eighteen minutes. Don't you hate that? So now I was rested and up. I would never get to sleep. I would never see the sun. I would never see Victoria.

I got out of bed and turned on my computer to send e-mail, GirlWar to QueenV3.

I meant to ask her if she was mad at me. If I said something wrong. I meant to write about soccer and Juwan Spenser. Shopping for school clothes. My stupid talk with Mom. I meant to ask a million questions about Nigeria. Instead all I wrote was "Glad you're back. Let's get together."

Now I could sleep. Really sleep.

The next time I woke up, streams of light beamed through my blinds. Sure enough, the sun was grinning at me, a big old cheesy grin. I was in and out of the shower so fast I didn't need a towel to dry off. That's how little water actually hit me. I know I brushed my teeth and threw on my soccer outfit. I just didn't do all of those grooming things on Mom's "did you" list. I scooted into my chair and kept my legs under the tablecloth to hide the fact that they were lotionless. Once I got to rolling around on the soccer field, no one would know the difference.

"Chew, Akilah. Ten times, then swallow."

"I *am* chewing." My mouth was all full of toast.

"Young lady! Close your mouth."

I'm no lady, I thought. I'm just a girl, ready to kick butt on the soccer field—after I see Victoria.

When I ran to the Ojikes' house, Miss Lady was out walking Gigi. The second the dog caught scent of me, Gigi started barking like mad. Miss Lady didn't yank Gigi's leash or quiet her down. She just let her bark.

"I see you ain't waste no time making it over here." Miss Lady saw everything. "Is your mama well, child?"

"My mama's fine," I said.

"How'd she let you out the house with those ashy legs?"

"I'm going to play soccer in the grass and mud. I'ma have to take a bath when I come home anyway."

"You can still fix up. Be a lady," she said. Now Gigi was sniffing me. I didn't care about Gigi's wet snout as much as I cared about people insisting I be a lady. I'm a girl, not a lady.

I went up to the Ojikes' door and pressed the buzzer. I rocked back and forth, feeling like I could lift off and fly. The excitement of finally seeing Victoria was killing me, but I managed to keep my feet on the ground.

Mrs. Ojike opened the door. I had to look up. Really up, because Mrs. Ojike is, as Mom says, "a woman of stature."

"So early, Akilah."

"Couldn't wait," I said. "I'm so glad you all are back." I talked on and on but noticed she wasn't letting me in, nor did she stand aside.

"I'm sorry, Akilah, but Victoria is not feeling well."

"Can't I see her for a minute? Just a minute? Please?"
I dragged out the *please*.

"Dear, she's not yet awake."

"It's not like I've never seen her pj's before."

I tried to look past Mrs. Ojike, but she didn't give me
an inch in either direction. The door was cracked wide
enough for her figure alone.

"Well, I'll be back tomorrow."

"Akilah, Victoria is not well. You must give her time
to feel better."

I knew I was wearing out my welcome, but I thought
she'd change her mind.

I went to the soccer field. During the warm-ups I was
minding my business, stretching with Janetta Mitchell,
when Juwan came over and said, "So where's your ugly
partner hiding?"

That was a trick to make me answer. Then he'd say, "I
told you Victoria's ugly." I had to fall for that trick only
once to know better. I said, "Juwan, you're the only ugly
person I know." Janetta and I kept doing our warm-ups
until he went away.

Juwan has known me since Pre-K. Same amount of
time he's known Janetta Mitchell. Does he bother *her*? No.

After practice I started on my way home. I took
Victoria's block, hoping I'd see her or Nelson out in the
yard.

Just as I was willing Victoria or Nelson to come outside, Mrs. Ojike opened the front door and called out to me. I raced over like a bloodhound. So much for being a lady.

Just as I got to the porch, she said, "Wait right here," and closed the door. I thought she was bringing Victoria to the door to say a quick hello. Instead she returned with a shopping bag that she put in my hand, closing my fingers around the handle.

"It's for your mother."

"Oh."

"Run along, Akilah. I will let you know when Victoria is feeling better."

I took the bag home and gave it to Mom. She pulled out the cloth, squealed, and said, "It's beautiful!"

It was just a cloth. Not like the *kente* Mrs. Ojike had on her wall. This one didn't have all of those colors laced into one another. It was just brown and black, with some white stick figure drawings on it.

Mom kept running her hands along the patterns. "It's a mud cloth," she said, her eyes darting from wall to wall. She was finding the perfect spot to hang it.

I didn't care where it went. As I slumped, sulking, on the sofa, I heard the words *texture* and *print* and *glorious*.

"Hey."

My head stayed sunken in my hands.

"I thought we'd have to pry you from the Ojikes."

"Mrs. Ojike said Victoria wasn't feeling well. Not to come by tomorrow, either. Don't call us. We'll call you."

"She didn't say that."

Mom sat down. She pulled my back braid to lift my head up out of my hands. I let my head drop back down.

"Akilah, listen to me. You have to give Victoria time. Maybe she didn't adapt to her country. Maybe it was too much for her."

I looked up. "Adapt?"

"Sure, Victoria was born in Nigeria, but she's lived in England and in Queens for most of her life. I'm sure the food, the water, the travel, perhaps even the climate, overwhelmed her."

I didn't want to hear it, but I knew Mom was probably right.

"Akilah."

I looked up.

"Those ashy legs, young lady."

Cousins

Mom and Dad did everything they could to distract me from missing Victoria. Honest to God, it would have been easier if they had given me a brother or sister six years ago when I asked for one. How many video games can you play and how much hoops can you shoot with your dad?

Finally my parents put me out of my misery when Mom announced, "We're going down to Silver Spring to see your cousins."

Silver Spring, Maryland, is six hours from Queens if we leave in the middle of the night and forever if we wait for the morning. I know the trip like I know my way to school, but I still anticipated going down to see my cousins. I love every inch of the long ride. The blue signs that point to rest stops. The green signs that subtract miles as we near Silver Spring. I love cruising neck and neck with other vacation-bound cars, and vanloads of kids fighting in backseats. I love the sing-alongs song after song. The radio stations crackling and disappearing as we cross from state to state. The car-counting game,

Spot That License Plate, and the spelling games. Then a long round of remember when . . . ? That always comes from Mom, because Dad never remembers anything correctly.

I love being around Mom's six sisters, who all live in Maryland. Her brother, my only blood uncle, lives in D.C., away from his sisters—Aunties Cassandra, Jackie, Lena, Lorna, Myra, and Belinda. Can you imagine that? Uncle Jason in the midst of seven girls.

Unlike my uncle, Daddy loves the fuss my aunties make over him. He doesn't really have a family. His mother died when he was little, and his father gave him away. When we say we're going to visit relatives, we mean Mom's side of the family.

We always stay at Aunt Cassandra's house. She's Mom's oldest sister and inherited Grandma and Grandpa's house, which has lots of room.

Auntie Cass is funny. Not ha-ha-trying-to-make-you-laugh funny, but funny. She never has two minutes to think about what's on her mind, so she just says whatever.

I expected my cousins to all come running out to greet us when we drove up, but not a soul appeared from the house. Not even the dog. Dad gave Mom a glance as we got out of the car. *Didn't they know we were coming?*

We went around the back. The windows were wide open, and we could hear Auntie Cass whipping one of my cousins and saying in between each stroke, "See—if—I'm—playing—with—you."

Mom hollered up, "Cass! Cass!" I think she did that more to stop the whipping than to announce we were there. Mom calls whipping child abuse.

First there was the silence of things stopping. Then footsteps. A troop of them bounding downstairs. Auntie Cass stuck her head out the window.

"Baby? Is that you?"

Five of my cousins and the dog all came running down to greet us.

Auntie Cass has the biggest family of all my aunts. Her oldest daughter is married with a family of her own. The two after her are in college, and the rest of my six cousins are still at home. Since five cousins had come down all dry eyed and giddy, I knew Pearlina was upstairs nursing her sore tail, which sucked raw eggs, because she's my age and I hang out with her the most.

I was glad we had passed by all of those restaurants along the way without going in. We had come just in time for breakfast and were going to be fed like nobody's business. Hot pans are always sizzling on Auntie Cass's stove. Don't get me wrong. My mother cooks at home, but not like Auntie Cass. Auntie starts off mornings with big, hot breakfasts, then around four o'clock she serves supper. She always puts out enough food to hurt your stomach. At eight o'clock there are leftovers, and after that there's cake or peach cobbler if you are good.

I didn't think I'd eat again at four, but I couldn't help myself. All of that good food and everybody laughing and eating! I wanted Pearlina to come downstairs and join in all the fun. Twice I stood outside her door knocking, but she wouldn't answer me. I could hear her sniffling.

I never took Pearlina to be the sensitive type. On that first day I gave up on her and ran around with my other cousins.

By the eight o'clock leftovers, my other aunties had come over with their husbands and kids, so the house was loud and happy.

Vanilla ice cream was being scooped on top of plates of peach cobbler. I dug into my mound of slurpy goodness, knowing I'd be sick that night, but I didn't care. I just kept on eating, much to my mother's embarrassment.

Mom wasn't really digging into her food. At least not like Dad, who was ready for seconds. She had stuff on her mind. It was in her stare. Mom wouldn't let the day go by without having her say.

I counted backward. Ten, nine, eight . . .

Mom put down her spoon and said, "Cass, you know I don't approve of physical punishment—"

"Look, Baby," Auntie Cass said, while washing the dishes. No one in Mom's family calls my mother Gladys, which was also my grandmother's name. "Wrong is wrong. You do wrong, you get what's coming. I raised six of you girls and Jason, plus nine of my own. No one died from a whipping yet."

That's what I meant by funny.

Dad must have laughed the loudest, which didn't please Mom at all. Auntie Cass is his favorite sister-in-law. He answered her like she was the captain and he was a lowly shipmate. In turn, Auntie Cass complained that Mom didn't cook enough for Dad. "Look at poor Roy. He's all bone."

Auntie Jackie always takes up for Mom. "Now, Roy," she said to Dad. "How are you taking Cass's side when she didn't want Baby to marry you?"

Before we knew it, my aunts were telling the story of my parents' courtship, which Dad seemed to enjoy. Well, more than Mom did. Neither Grandpa Jack nor Grandma Gladys thought my father would know how to treat a wife and kids since he didn't grow up in a real family himself. My mother had to prove everyone wrong and went ahead and married my father anyway.

Mom wouldn't let her sisters change the subject before she spoke out against whippings. Her workdays had been spent with kids who were beaten or abused. These same abused kids learned to beat up other kids and eventually turned on their own parents and children. To my mother, Auntie Cassandra said, "Baby, sounds like you need to change jobs."

Just like that, everyone was laughing.

"You'll see," Aunt Cass promised. "One day you'll have to crack the whip on that little tail"—she pointed to me—"and you'll be glad you did."

All my aunties started to laugh and tell stories about either the worst whippings they got as children or the worst whippings they gave as parents. And then my cousins proudly told stories of how they hid under beds and did the whipping dance when the belt lashed out at their legs and feet. After a while even Mom couldn't help herself and was laughing along with everyone else.

Then my cousin Pearlina came downstairs. When I saw her face and how she reached out to me from across the room without saying a word, I began to miss Victoria again.

Ready for the Fifth Grade

Finally! First day of school. Visiting my cousins was fun, but I wanted the summer to end and for things to go back to normal. I was ready to sit next to Victoria in our new class and shoot our hands in the air to get our new teacher's attention.

I wasn't the only one anxious for the summer to end. Mom decided she was well rested and ready to return to work. I think once Auntie Cass suggested she should change jobs, Mom had to prove her big sister wrong. Whatever had happened to make her leave her job now made her determined to go back to it. I was glad to see Mom in her heels and work clothes. When I was little and asked her where was she going, she used to say, "I'm going to rescue children."

The morning was perfect, all bright and chirpy. Mrs. Ojike couldn't keep Victoria in the house forever. Whatever Victoria had, the flu or an earache, had to be over by now. I couldn't wait to go over there and grab Victoria. Both of us would go running down the street, ready for fifth grade, our braids flying and us laughing. It doesn't take much to set us off. I'll look at her big teeth or she'll see my big head and we'll burst out laughing so hard we gotta cough, then slap each other on the back.

As if my thoughts were sitting out on the table next to the jelly, Mom said, "Mrs. Ojike took Victoria to school this morning. She called to tell me."

Pow. Right in the gut.

Mom offered to take me to school. But I knew she'd be late for work.

She was feeling sorry for me, which made it worse. We're alike, Mom and I. We can't stand pity. We don't want to get it and we don't want to give it. There you are being sympathetic, waiting for the other person to snap out of it, but they're content to ride pity like it's the rocking horse you feed quarters into. Take Cousin Pearlina. I spent the first day pleading with her to let me inside her room. Then it was three whole days before she spoke without tears welling up in her eyes. By the time she was herself again, we had to come back to Queens.

"It's only a couple of blocks," I told Mom, who was still heaping on the pity look. "I'll walk."

When I got to the playground, I started looking for Victoria, searching among the clap-clap games and hopscotches. It was wild out there. Just wild. Kids who had been locked up in their homes all summer and kids who hadn't seen one another for months were finally out—screaming, running, and having a ball. All the colors of new school clothes darted this way and that. Then the bell rang and everyone scattered, trying to figure out which line they belonged to. It was while the playground was going motion crazy that I found her, sitting still and alone against the chain-link fence, her face turned away from the playground.

I ran over to get her.

"Victoria! Victoria! Come on!" I grabbed her hand and pulled her to Ms. Saunders's line. It didn't matter that her feet were dragging like I was pulling her through mud. I could fly for the both of us. I squeezed her hand and ran, laughing all the way. I thought we were both laughing, but I heard mostly me. I was too excited to notice anything else. When we got on line, I kept saying, "Hi, hi, hi."

She said hi back, or her mouth opened to say hi. We weren't supposed to be talking on line anyway, but I was bursting all over. Inside and out. Finally. Victoria and me. Back together again.

I glanced over at the boys' line just to see which boys would be in our class, and man! There was Juwan Spenser. He is like an embarrassing nickname that follows you everywhere. I can't get rid of him. That boy followed me from Pre-K to first, second, and fourth grades, plus soccer practice. The third grade was my only break. I went to 3–1 and he went to 3–2. Well, I wasn't going to waste my time thinking about Juwan Spenser and what misery he could cause me. I was too happy to be standing next to Victoria.

Our new class, 5–2, marched behind our teacher, Ms.

Saunders, down the hall, up the stairwell, and into our new classroom. There we found the usual rows of desks, and on each desk was a small name card made of construction paper.

"Find your names and take your seats."

I panicked. The problem with a lightning-quick mind is you jump ahead. What if Ms. Saunders alphabetized our names? *A* for Akilah would put me on the other side of the world from *V* for Victoria. *H* for Hunter still had no hope of being close to *O*, Ojike. Victoria might as well still be in Nigeria.

Breathe, girl. Breathe.

I calmed myself and scanned the cards around me. I saw that our names had not been alphabetized and that only Jerilyn Miller kept me from sitting next to Victoria. Once again Girl Warrior rose up. I switched the name cards and took my place next to Victoria. Jerilyn didn't care one way or the other.

Now I was ready for the fifth grade.

Geography Game

Ms. Saunders said we would play a geography game to see who had traveled farthest over the summer. Although the grand prize would go to the one who went the farthest, there would be other prizes for most unique travel.

"We will play by process of elimination." Ms. Saunders's accent sounded both familiar and different. Her long words were neat at the beginnings and ends but lilted in the middles. She was from a Caribbean island, although I couldn't pinpoint which one.

I didn't have a chance of winning, but I wanted to play as long as I could. At least Victoria had a real shot. She had just returned from Africa. West Africa. Nigeria. Unless someone traveled to East Africa or South Africa or China, Victoria had the prize in the bag.

We all stood up.

"Who left Queens this summer?" Ms. Saunders asked, surveying the room. She wore round glasses with lenses that magnified her eyes, which meant those eyes didn't miss a thing. Even so, she had "nice teacher" written all over her. I could tell she was the kind of teacher who loved smart kids and was patient with the Juwan Spensers of the world.

Three of my classmates were the first to be eliminated. They hadn't gone anywhere over the summer. Not even to the pier for the Fourth of July, to Yankee Stadium for a ball game, or to Bear Mountain for a picnic.

Ms. Saunders then asked, "Has anyone left the state of New York?" She circled the green pork chop on the map. By the time she turned away from the map, Juwan Spenser and half of the class had sat down.

Jerilyn Miller raised her hand. "Ms. Saunders, does going to a funeral in New Jersey count for out of state?" Jerilyn knew full well New Jersey was a state of its own. We were in Mrs. Ryan's class last year, and Mrs. Ryan drilled us about the fifty states, the capitals, and their flowers. You couldn't be promoted unless you knew them.

Then Ritchie Lewis asked if surfing on the Internet counted. If it did, he went rock climbing in Colorado, coral reef diving in Maui, and gliding through the Everglades.

Region by region, Ms. Saunders eliminated us, decorating the map with pushpins to mark the places we traveled to. She asked if anyone had traveled south of the Mason-Dixon line. I tried to pretend I didn't know what she meant, but my face gave me away.

Why couldn't my cousins live in Alabama like Janetta Mitchell's family or in Mississippi like Kyla's family? Silver Spring, Maryland, wasn't far south enough. I hated that my chances of winning were over, even though I knew I would have been eliminated sooner or later. At least Victoria was still standing, I thought. I could root for her.

No one had gone farther west than Chicago, which was where Nahda went for vacation. Ms. Saunders then stuck red pushpins in Puerto Rico, the Dominican Republic, Jamaica, and Trinidad, the countries where Carmen, Fedelina, Thurston, and Vincent visited. She also stuck a pin in Barbados, which is where she went for the summer to see her family.

Now only three players stood: Victoria, Zuhair, and Ida. I realized Victoria wasn't going to win. Zuhair's family was from Yemen and Ida's family was from the Philippines.

Ms. Saunders asked Victoria which continent she traveled to—as if she couldn't guess.

Victoria said, "Africa," the first clear word I'd heard her speak since she came back.

Ms. Saunders got that "motherland" look that pushed her moon face out even rounder. I know that look all too well because my mother often wears it when she's proud of and excited about all things African.

I glanced at Victoria. Have you ever seen that old photo of Queen Victoria in an encyclopedia? The one where she's wearing a black dress, with a high, stiff collar, and her face is bulldog proud? That's sort of like Victoria's natural expression, which she copied from Queen Victoria, her heroine. But Victoria didn't seem especially proud like the queen of England. She seemed nervous.

Ms. Saunders didn't know Victoria looked different. How could she? Ms. Saunders was still excited about Victoria's trip to Africa and asked which countries she visited. Before Victoria could answer, Ms. Saunders said, "Class, Africa is made up of how many countries?"

It was kind of funny to see a teacher act so giddy. Ms. Saunders must really love Africa.

I shot my hand up along with my classmates'. My face pleaded to be called on, especially when every number from twenty to two hundred was shouted out. Finally Ms. Saunders looked my way, searching for my name card that had fallen on the floor. She glanced at her attendance book, pointed, and said, "Jerilyn."

I scooped up my name card and said, "I'm Akilah. We switched. And there are more than fifty countries and about seven hundred million people."

"Why, thank you, Akilah," Ms. Saunders said. "Living up to the meaning of your name." She winked at me, rather than tell the class that *Akilah* means "intelligent" in Swahili. I winked back.

Ms. Saunders said, "I began my teaching career in Kenya. Throughout the year, I will share many interesting facts about my experiences there." She circled Kenya on the map. Then she returned her attention to Victoria. "Which country did you visit"—she looked at her name card—"Victoria?"

Victoria didn't answer, so Ms. Saunders repeated herself.

Finally Victoria said, "Nigeria."

Ms. Saunders was even more excited. "And was there a special reason for the trip?" She stuck a green pushpin in the heart of Nigeria. When her back was turned, I thought I heard Victoria say, "To die." Or maybe it was my imagination.

Victoria shook her head no.

Head shake? Head shake? Victoria wasn't a head shaker or a mumbler, for that matter. The know-it-all in me almost shot up my arm to answer, "There was a special celebration to mark her coming-of-age," but I used my self-control. That was especially hard, having the answer ready.

"May I sit?" Victoria asked.

Two girls, whose names I did not know, mimicked her. They weren't in the fourth grade with us last year. They didn't know that Victoria was born in Nigeria and lived in England until she was eight and spoke like the queen.

Girl Warrior gave them both a mean look: *If you mess with her, you mess with me.* They got it and shut up.

Ms. Saunders let Victoria take her seat. That left Zuhair and Ida still standing.

No Laughter

We had to write an essay for language arts. Just a paragraph or two of suggestions about improving the environment so Ms. Saunders could "assess our writing skills." I couldn't contain myself. Two paragraphs? I covered every line on my paper, front and back.

Even though our first essay wouldn't be graded, I was anxious to get mine back to read Ms. Saunders's comments. Just like she was checking us out, I was checking her out too.

When we got our essays back, I looked over at Victoria's paper, partly because I wanted to compare Ms. Saunders's comments and partly because I missed Victoria's loopty-loo *L*s and jolly *P* stems.

First I tried to look on the sly, but Victoria didn't make it easy. Her handwriting was tiny and scrunched together in secret code letters. She hadn't even written entire lines from left to right. Instead, her two paragraphs looked like the Japanese poems we studied in Mrs. Ryan's class, two and three words to a line.

On top of her paper Ms. Saunders wrote, *Victoria,*

margins? Paragraphs? Topic? See me. I had no trouble reading those words. Big. Red. Slanting to the right. Each word ending in fishhooks.

For once I didn't care about our little competition. From those big red letters, the *See me,* and those fishhooks, I knew Victoria was in trouble. Ms. Saunders had already "assessed" that Victoria's writing skills weren't up to fifth-grade standards.

Victoria didn't seem bothered by all that red writing on her paper. She just opened her loose-leaf binder and neatly slipped the essay into the language arts section.

I panicked for both of us. I couldn't let Mrs. Ojike see that paper. Victoria never brought home a grade less than a Very Good. Mental note: Rip out that essay the minute we leave the school yard.

In math we were doing review, and I had rocket arm so bad Ms. Saunders stopped calling on me. Juwan mouthed a cuss at me, but Ms. Saunders caught him and made him write, "Intelligent people do not curse" on both sides of a sheet of paper that his mother would have to sign. I couldn't wait to get out on the playground to laugh, laugh, laugh at his sorry buzzard head.

"To figure out Jerry's average score, we must . . ." Ms. Saunders circled the room with her eyes. "Who haven't I heard from—Victoria Ojike. What a lovely name."

Of course everyone snickered. Don't teachers know when they're embarrassing you?

Victoria was looking ahead but not up at Ms.

Saunders, like she was doing a trick: How to pretend you're there when you're not.

Her mouth parted. She might have even said, "Yes?" but it was so low.

Ms. Saunders stood directly before Victoria's row, tapping her foot. Victoria's trick would not work this time.

"Victoria, are you with us?"

A voice in the back of the classroom said, "She's in outer space."

Juwan—as if he weren't already in enough trouble—joined in. "She's in the deepest, darkest Congo."

I hated him and he knew it. He just gave me one big headache.

Ms. Saunders raised an eyebrow in Juwan and Darryl's direction and the room got quiet. Ms. Saunders is such a nice lady, but when she becomes stern you know better than to mess with her. As if nothing had happened, she turned to Victoria with her moon pie face. Soft. Patient.

"Victoria," she said, "what operation will we perform first?"

Then I saw it! The word *operation* made Victoria's eyes jump.

"Operation?"

Ms. Saunders seemed truly dumbfounded. She wondered what I was wondering. Was this Victoria Ojike from 4–1? Mathorama champ? First runner-up in last year's spelling bee?

Janetta called, "First you add up all of his scores, then you divide." Ms. Saunders made the raise-your-hand gesture. Janetta raised her hand then blurted out her answer.

Before the dismissal buzzer sounded, Ms. Saunders reminded Victoria that she wanted to speak to her. I tried to linger behind, but Ms. Saunders cleared her throat and told me to get going. I stood outside the closed door until Mrs. Jenkins, the hall aide, showed me the way out.

I must have waited outside for thirty minutes. Almost every bus and van had left by the time Victoria finally came shlushing through the doors. That's exactly how she walked. Kind of draggy, like she was shlushing through puddles in galoshes.

"What did she say?" I asked.

"Say?"

"I hate when you do that and you do it a lot," I said. "Ms. Saunders. What did she say?"

She took a few draggy steps before she said, "Nothing."

"Nothing?" Now I was doing it. "Ms. Saunders didn't say 'Akilah, beat it' to tell you nothing. What she say?"

Victoria shrugged.

If she didn't talk, my imagination was only going to take off. I already had a few ideas while watching the last bus pull off. I pictured Ms. Saunders saying, "Victoria, if you don't snap out of it I will be forced to put you in the slow class." Or "Victoria, I am going to change your seat so I can watch you better."

Victoria wouldn't even look at me. She just kept

walking slow. I'd walk slow too if I had to show my mother all that red writing on my paper.

Sooner or later she'd have to tell me what was going on. In the meantime I changed the subject so we could laugh about how Juwan got snagged for cursing in class. I was starting to go on about Juwan's haircut when Victoria said, "Don't do that."

"What?"

"Try to make me laugh."

Well, now I was mad. "Excuse me, Queen Victoria. Off with my head, why doncha?"

"That's from *Alice in Wonderland*, and it's not funny."

"First you say don't make you laugh. Then you say I'm not funny. Girl, you better make up your mind."

She stopped right there, pushed her finger in my chest, and said like she was a crossing guard, "No laughter."

"What?"

She said, "You can't make me laugh. No one can. So do not try."

Why did she have to dare me? Daring me was like waving a red cape at a bull. I knew exactly how to make her laugh. I reached to tickle the sensitive skin under her chin to prove it. She slapped my hand away, hard.

I slapped her back. Harder.

We just stood there, eye to eye, neither one of us speaking or blinking. Then she walked away.

Sulking

When Dad tried to jolly me with a trip to the video store, Mom said, "Leave her alone. She's sulking. Let her sulk."

Dad wasn't hearing Mom at all. He said, "Let's shoot some hoops, baby girl. I'll spot you eight points."

I shook my head no. Then *he* started to sulk, which annoyed me because there wasn't room for his sulking. Only mine. And on top of that, I had a headache. One that had been creeping up the back of my head for a while. I had the exact same headache last month at the start of the half moon. I knew, because the first time my head throbbed like this, I opened my window so I could howl at the moon, *arroOUUU*. There was the moon, with its face turned sideways, laughing at me.

Dad wouldn't let things be. He was still trying to get me to open up. "Bad day at school, puddin'?"

Mom got annoyed. "Roy."

He wouldn't let go. "Someone giving you a hard time? Is it that Juwan character?" He turned to Mom and said, "That boy thinks he can get away with it because she's an *only*. There's always strength in numbers on the playground, Gladys."

Out of nowhere, Mom and Dad's ongoing argument, the one they think I can't hear at night, worked its way into the living room. It's all about the baby Dad wants Mom to have before they get too old. Dad doesn't believe that I should grow up alone. Mom answered, "Fine, Roy. I'll have another baby if you stay home to take care of it." After that Dad was excited like a kid on Christmas Eve and started making plans to work at home. Mom saw her reverse psychology hadn't worked and told him she wasn't having any more kids. She said there were too many kids in the world as it was.

I wanted to go upstairs before they made my headache worse.

Dad told me, "If I have to escort you to school each and every day, I will."

I wouldn't talk. My head was killing me and I was mad at Victoria. I just wanted to be in my room with the door closed.

My refusal to talk only made Dad more concerned. "Akilah, I'm your dad," he coaxed. "If there's anything I should know about, you can tell me."

Now I knew how Victoria felt when I kept bugging her, then trying to jolly her. I was still mad at her, but I understood.

"Dad, I don't feel like talking," I said.

"Is it girl stuff?"

I screamed. I didn't know Girl Warrior had an ounce

of sissy in her, but boy did it come out.

Mom told Dad what movie she wanted to rent, then pushed him out the door. Literally. I braced myself for some slicker interrogation from my mom. After all, she's a pro at getting kids to open up. She deals with kids who clam up after seeing or going through horrible stuff. But today she did the unexpected. She fixed me a cup of chamomile tea with lots of honey and broke a Tylenol in half for my headache. Then she went upstairs to her room and closed the door.

My headache was gone by the next morning, but that feeling of things not being right between Victoria and me was still there. I thought we'd have an awkward moment when we sat down at our desks, but she didn't even look my way. Not once. Well, two could play that game, I thought. If our fight didn't bother her, I wouldn't let it bother me.

For the next couple of days I stuck with Janetta and my other friends. I expected Victoria to play jacks with Nahda or Sadia, her other friends, but she stayed by herself during recess and lunchtime.

We still didn't say boo to each other. Not when we passed dittos from left to right or when we corrected each other's spelling quizzes. When I thought about it long enough, I concluded that sitting next to Victoria was like it had been since the first day of school. She took her seat, handed in her homework, copied down the lessons, and stared ahead like she was listening, although I knew she was doing her "present but absent" trick. By the end of the week, I thought, if she turned my way first, I would say hi, but she just kept doing her trick.

I couldn't help but notice that Victoria, Miss Mathorama, never volunteered to solve problems at the board, nor did she raise her hand, or laugh at anything. Not even when Ms. Saunders read a nonsense poem that was so hilarious that Ms. Saunders giggled through half of it. And even while everyone was laughing, I caught Ms. Saunders doing what I had been doing: checking out Victoria.

Falling off a Cliff

Ms. Saunders needed a volunteer to clap erasers and clean the blackboard, so I stuck my hand up. Not that I had to fight off anyone for the honor. She smiled at me, knowing I couldn't help myself.

"This shouldn't take too long," Ms. Saunders said as the class, including Victoria, filed out into the hallway. "You might be able to catch up with your friends."

"Oh, that's okay," I said. "I'm in no hurry."

She was opening the lower window so I could stick the erasers out of it. Then she said, "Akilah, you're friends with Victoria," in a leading-up-to way.

"Not really," I said.

She didn't believe me. Isn't it funny how a person can communicate a clear thought with one look?

I had to clarify. "We're not speaking."

"I see."

I pounded the erasers together, *bang, bang, ba-bang,* creating a cloud of chalk dust. It didn't bother me, but Ms. Saunders, who was a good ten feet away, started to cough.

"Sorry," I said.

She said it was all right, but didn't ask any more questions about Victoria and me.

I didn't have to pass by Victoria's house to go home. I could have made a U around the school, gone down Henley Road, then walked up to my house instead of going the usual route. I could have taken the long way, the avoiding-Victoria way, but I wouldn't. I was not the guilty one. Instead I was defiant. I was proud. My giant steps proclaimed I was not the bad friend.

I was walking my defiant walk, feeling proud, when I saw Nelson entering the Ojikes' yard.

Nelson doesn't take my breath away. I breathe just fine when he is near. Instead, my legs slide out from under me, and my arms want to flutter. Like I'm both falling off a cliff and floating in the air, like riding the Cyclone at Coney Island, but in slow motion.

Nelson is the first boy I truly, truly liked. He's sixteen. Practically a man. He stands taller than Mr. Ojike, which is amazing all by itself. Mr. Ojike is at least six feet and Dad is five ten. So, yeah. Nelson is taller than my father.

Nelson's teeth are white and even. When he smiles, those white teeth against all that chocolate, unh, unh, unh! Back when we were friends, I told Victoria that I was going to marry Nelson so we could be sisters, but that was a lie. Nelson is going to be mine for the sake of being mine. He is better than any boy I know, so why waste my time having silly crushes on boys who are not Nelson?

I plain old love Nelson. Know how much? I organized a protest against school uniforms when they sent home notices announcing that our school was considering navy pleated skirts and white shirts with fake neckties. Of course Girl Warrior swung into action. I wrote up my own petition and collected signatures at Shop-Rite and after church. I even sent e-mail to the local newspapers that said, "Why should we all look alike? Think alike? Be alike?" And then the Ojikes moved into the neighborhood and I saw Nelson standing tall in his school uniform: a navy blazer, a white shirt, tan pants, and a real necktie. Unh, unh, unh. I dropped my petition and my e-mails against school uniforms right then and there.

On Saturdays Victoria and I used to go to the park to watch Nelson play football (which was actually rugby) with other Africans who live around our way. We'd sit in the grass and guard Nelson's stuff, and we rooted like fools no matter what he did. Then he'd jog over for his water bottle, which I held onto. He'd squeeze the bottle, swallow, then toss it back to me.

And his accent! British like the Prince of Wales, except when he speaks to his parents. Then he speaks in a Yoruba dialect. Nelson is very twenty-first century and traditional at the same time.

"How do I find you alone, Akilah?"

Tell me I didn't feel silly! I held myself together and just shrugged.

"Where is your shadow?"

"You tell me," I said. "She quit me first."

"A falling out." He said this so seriously, but I knew he wasn't taking me seriously at all.

"Should I fetch Victoria? She might already be inside."

I couldn't look at Nelson without seeing Victoria. I wanted to stay mad at her, but I was now more puzzled than mad. Kinda like Ms. Saunders, trying to put it all together. If anyone knew why Victoria didn't want to laugh or shoot her hand up in class like in the good old days, Nelson did.

"Why's Victoria acting so strange?"

He repeated back, "Strange?" although he knew what I meant. He was just stalling. He couldn't fool me. Just before they left for Africa, I conducted my own personal study on Nelson Ojike so I wouldn't forget one detail about him. I spilled all my Nelson data inside my journal, using the pages for June second through the fourteenth. I know every look on his face. Every tone in his voice. Every polo shirt he owns.

"She won't laugh. Don't want to laugh. She keeps to herself. And she writes in really tiny letters."

"Ah!" he said, like a lightbulb had flashed on. "She is getting over illness. She'll soon be herself."

It was the first time I saw his teeth smiling at me that I didn't have that deep-down Nelson love hurling me like the Coney Island Cyclone. Nelson was lying to me. Every inch of me knew it. My legs stayed firmly under me and my arms didn't feel like flying. I hadn't completely fallen out of love with Nelson, but once I knew he was lying to me, I wasn't hardly falling off of no cliff.

Sorry

When your one true friend makes you mad, you think you will never have another friend. You will have a poodle before you have another friend—and poodles are nothing but trouble. I see how Gigi always has Miss Lady in circles trying to untangle the leash around her ankles.

That only made me remember stuff Victoria and I did together, like start a dog-walking business. We were all psyched to walk dogs around the park but hadn't thought who was going to pick up all that poop.

I decided to write Victoria a note. One word: *Sorry*. Someone had to take the first step, and my steps were bigger than hers.

This was hardly our first falling out. Shoot. We'd get mad, call each other names, insult each other's shoes and lopsided braids, then pretend that the other didn't exist. We'd get tired of acting out and would make excuses to be in each other's space. After one grin everything would go back to normal. No questions asked.

Don't get me wrong. I'm not one of those lonely girls

with only one friend in the world. I have friends. It's that Victoria is my one true friend. But not best friend. I don't like that term. Sooner or later the "best friend" tests you. "Who is your best friend, her or me?" Janetta Mitchell put me through that. She said, "You my best friend, Akilah. We been close since Pre-K." Then she wanted me to say it back, again and again. Victoria and I are different. We don't talk about being friends. We *are* friends. True friends.

We met two years ago at the playground. Her father worked in the Nigerian consulate's office. In fact, Miss Lady spread the rumor that the Nigerian government paid for the Ojikes' house and car. That only made Victoria seem more interesting to me.

"My name is Victoria" was how she introduced herself. When I said "I'll call you Vickie for short," she repeated herself: "My name is Victoria." She did not like for short.

I said, "Okay. If you insist."

She said, "I insist."

Then I said, "My name is African."

She looked at me square on, no blinking, no smiling, and said, "Hello, African."

I laughed, then said, "No, my name is Akilah. *It* is African." She said, "You said your name is African, so I called you by your name."

"Do you know what *Akilah* means?" I quizzed.

"Of course I do," Victoria said. "It means 'born when the hyena was laughing.'"

"Not hardly. It means 'intelligent.'"

"It means 'laughs like an intelligent hyena.'"

She said it so matter-of-factly that I couldn't stop laughing. Then she said, "See?"—not even cracking a smile.

"I am named for Queen Victoria. For the Victoria Falls, and Lake Victoria. Have you heard of Lake Victoria?"

If it is in Africa, I was sure I had. My mother surrounds me with all things African. I have dolls from thirty African countries. Mom taught me some Swahili, some African dances (which Victoria later laughed at), and gave me books on African history and geography. Somewhere I must have run across Lake Victoria.

"Why don't you have an African name?" I asked her.

"Why do you have an African name?"

"Don't answer with a question," I said.

"Don't question."

We clicked. From that moment I knew Victoria was the missing piece to my puzzle. She didn't say that typical "Yo' greasy granny" stuff like Juwan. She was like me, an individual, and not about to hide it. From then on it was always she and I.

During language arts, I used my best cursive letters to write the one word in the center of a paper. I tore it out of my loose-leaf binder, folded it down to a tight rectangle, and held onto it until the first warning bell rang.

Finally school was over, so I dropped the note on

Victoria's desk. I gave Victoria a chance to scoot out of her chair and walk with me, but she stayed seated, her head down.

I looked up. Mrs. Ojike was standing at the door. She wore a blue and yellow printed head wrap and matching dress that had this swirling white embroidery around the neckline. That was nothing. Nisha's mother drives up to the school wearing sandals and saris that show her belly even in the winter.

Ms. Saunders was going to give Mrs. Ojike the bad news: Victoria had to transfer to one of the slow classes.

I knew Mrs. Ojike had come in the nick of time. She was going to give Ms. Saunders some insight into Victoria's behavior. Maybe Victoria is forbidden to laugh after the age of ten. Now that I thought about it, Mrs. Ojike doesn't laugh. She smiles, but never breaks into a hearty haw-haw like my mother and aunties do.

Nelson laughs and Mr. Ojike laughs. But now Victoria would be like her mother and lose her laughter. Maybe becoming a lady in Nigeria is like becoming a lady here. Sit up straight, cross your legs, smile, and don't beat up boys in the park.

Ms. Saunders rose and beckoned Mrs. Ojike inside. I went up to greet her.

"Hi, Mrs. Ojike."

"Well, hello, Akilah." Mrs. Ojike looked down at me. It was weird, like looking at Victoria thirty years from now.

"Can I wait and walk home with y'all?" I had no

shame. My mother would have died if she had heard me.

"I'm afraid not today, dear. We will be a while."

I glanced back at Victoria, but her head was still down on her desk next to the note.

New Normal

By the next morning things were back to normal between Victoria and me. We walked to school together, then sat by the hopscotches until the bell rang. Whether I liked it or not, this was now normal. Not running down the street kicking a stone, our "in the meantime" soccer ball. Not laughing at each other's hairstyles, or treating each other to the word of the day. No. New normal meant we filled in space around each other. I did all the talking, not too much of it, and said nothing funny. She nodded, shrugged, or stared. I just sat with Victoria to make it seem like she wasn't alone.

Even though I didn't ask her about her mother's meeting with Ms. Saunders, I knew it helped. Victoria wrote in paragraphs instead of in Japanese poetry lines. Her letters weren't fat and loopy, but I could read them on her paper from my desk. She raised her hand at least once in language arts, science, and math to give short answers.

I wanted to believe these were all good signs, that Victoria was getting over her illness, as Nelson put it. But I knew that the girl sitting next to me wasn't the real

Victoria. She had just perfected her staring trick to include one-word answers. The real Victoria was famous for interjecting "Actually" to add more detail to our fourth-grade teacher's explanations. I liked that girl. She was a geek and not afraid to show it.

Ms. Saunders passed out the math dittos for homework. Three pages of them. It was all review, the same stuff I zipped through in workbooks over the summer, so I didn't care—unlike Juwan, who was having puppies. He pounded his fist on his desk and said, "Aw, man. Three sheets." I stuck my tongue out at him and Ms. Saunders caught me, so I had to write thirty times, "I will not taunt my fellow classmates." How fair was that? I'd have to write small and carefully to make it fit on one line.

I raised my hand. "Ms. Saunders, can't I just write 'I will not stick my tongue out'? I can make that fit easier. *Taunt*, *fellow*, and *classmates* will take too much room."

Ms. Saunders repeated the phrase "I will not taunt my fellow classmates" clearly, like I was hard of hearing. When the entire class, except for Victoria, laughed, Ms. Saunders got serious. First she hushed the class. Then she said, "Akilah, I want you to think about what taunting does and discuss it with your parents. Then summarize your findings and have your parents sign your sheet."

I felt Juwan's eyes dancing in his big clown head. I knew he wanted me to look his way, but I wouldn't give him any satisfaction.

Ms. Saunders held up another sheet of paper and said, "In two weeks we will begin a new and exciting discovery."

Discovery? A science word! Instantly I was healed from having been humiliated. I always knew science would get better in the fifth grade.

As sharp as my eyes were, I couldn't make out a single word on the yellow sheet, but I could see dotted lines, straight lines, and check boxes. These were all the things needed for a field trip. Already I could see an excavation site or a rock quarry, at the very least.

Ms. Saunders started a pile of yellow sheets at each row. We could barely contain our enthusiasm until she said, "We are going to learn about ourselves."

I, and the rest of my classmates, came crashing down with a thud.

"This is a permission form to attend sex education classes. Have your parents or guardian read this form, sign it, and return it to me. Some of your parents will want to teach this subject at home. That's okay," she said. "But if your parents check No, or if you do not return the signed permission slip, you will have library science during that period. Does anyone need it in a language other than English?"

Ms. Saunders had translations in Chinese, Spanish, and French, but she didn't have them in Hindi and Arabic. We had kids from all over.

Victoria and I walked home slowly, as we usually did. Her feet still shlushed along. I asked her, "Is your mother going to sign it?"

She shrugged. In the middle of missing her voice, I felt the thwack of a wet dart against the back of my neck.

Juwan stuck his head out of the bus window. "Gotcha, Akilah. I gotcha! Ha-ha!"

"Wait till tomorrow, Juwan!" I yelled, shaking my fist at him.

He yelled back, "I will not taunt my fellow classmates!" Then the bus pulled off.

I turned to Victoria. "That Juwan gets me so mad. He's going to get it."

She stared ahead and nodded.

Sitting Duck

Mom gave me a lecture about stooping to Juwan's level. After I wrote my punishment thirty times, she made me write a full-page essay about taunting instead of the summary Ms. Saunders asked for. She said, "None of this talking out of your head, Akilah. I want actual examples about the effects of taunting." Then I had to rewrite it for neatness before she signed it.

Dad said, "Gladys, lighten up. If Juwan Spenser was involved, I'm sure Akilah was provoked and couldn't help herself."

I smiled at my daddy. Yeah. I know I'm the princess and I was loving it—even though it didn't save me from having to write a full page.

As far as Mom was concerned, my self-esteem could have used a little grounding. She said, "How Juwan's mother raised him is her business. It doesn't have to rub off on my child."

I had almost forgotten about the permission slip, but there it was, in my backpack. "Oh, yeah. Sex education class," I said, pushing the form toward Mom.

"Sex education?" Dad asked. "You're in elementary school."

Mom gave Dad a look like she wanted to stick out her tongue and sing, "Nah-nah-nah-nah-nah." She signed her name with large, sharp strokes, grinning at Dad all the while. "She's not a baby, Roy."

Poor Daddy. He looked so betrayed. I'll bet he didn't know about our backyard tea talks.

When we were alone, Mom said, "Akilah, I was going to wait until you needed them, but there's no use holding onto these. Besides, you should be prepared."

You know how my mind takes off, just soars into flight? Instantly I pictured every wonderful surprise that she could have had waiting for me. But the ruby stud earrings in Mom's jewelry box, the ones I used to hold up to my naked earlobes, turned out to be a pack of sanitary napkins. A stupid starter kit.

I didn't put the sack of napkins in my drawer like Mom suggested. Instead I tossed them up in my closet, way back where I couldn't see them.

Don't get me wrong. I wasn't against getting my period. I just wanted to get mine when Victoria got hers so we could talk about it and compare notes. I needed Victoria to be with me, as in *present*, and not doing her staring-into-space trick.

There had to be a way to delay my period and buy us more time. At least six to eight months. If Mom was right and I started early, then I was a sitting duck. As it was, I had less than four months before my eleventh birthday.

Not that I thought I'd magically get it on my birthday. I wasn't that naive. But if I could get it closer to twelve, which was when most of the sixth graders got it, then Victoria and I had a better chance of both getting it the same year. The last thing I wanted was to get it at ten. We wouldn't be going through it together. It would be like she was in Nigeria and I was in Queens.

I went on-line to do a search and typed in *minstruation,* but not one article popped up from the web. On a second try I spelled it correctly and got over 600,000 hits. Can you believe that? The Internet was chock-full of articles on what people talked about in private. There were tons of medical articles with diagrams and statistics, and all the different names for periods. Then there were postings from girls writing about first periods and embarrassing period moments. None of this stuff was what I was look-ing for, so I kept on searching. The deeper I searched, the kookier it got. There were myths about periods and even celebration rituals. Hah! I'd never let my mother know about that. Mom loves rituals. I should know. I had an African naming ceremony and my umbilical cord was buried in the backyard. You name the ritual, Mom insists we do it. I understand, though. After her sisters went through everything, no one made a fuss when it was Mom's turn—except when she wanted to marry Dad.

I just kept clicking on links, looking for clues. Anything I could use to delay my period. So far my best shot was to become a super-duper athlete and exercise nonstop like a maniac. But there were no guarantees that that would work. If I was lucky, I might just get an irregular period, which I wasn't too sure I wanted.

I was about sixteen screens away from my first search. Somehow, from *menstruation* to *menses* to *lunar calendar*, I had landed on the moon.

I understood about the lunar calendar: how it takes a little over twenty-eight days for the arrival of a full moon, and that a period is supposed to come every twenty-eight days. Then there are blue moons, two full moons in one month. Did that mean you could get your period twice in a month? Yikes.

Instead of clicking back, I went forward and plunged deeper into stuff about how full moons can affect the number of babies being born. And that the moon causes tidal waves. And the *Apollo* astronauts walked on the moon. And people were auctioning off pieces of the moon. And there are more songs written about the moon than the sun. It was all driving me crazy. From sanitary napkins to the dark side of the moon. I was confused. My eyes were tired from jumping from stupid article to stupid article. None of this information was helping me.

I logged off and got into bed. I lay on my back, looking up at the moon through the venetian blind slats. A full moon hung outside my window. I yawned, closed my eyes, and fell into that heavy sleep, then *POW*! The clue I'd been searching for hit me, and I sprang right up.

The moonbeams. The moonbeams through my blinds. They were aimed right at me. Not just at me, but at my belly, where everything was.

I rolled away from the moonbeams.

It was no accident that I had landed on the moon. The clues were all there. The moon creates a tidal wave. A deep gravitational pull. If the moon could rock a tidal wave and cause more births, couldn't it pull down a period? Weren't periods based on the comings and goings of the moon? Didn't an Internet article say girls can get their period twice a month when there are two moons?

All this time I was bringing down my own period, sleeping directly under the moon, helping it pull, pull, pull on me.

I jumped out of bed and ran into a corner and balled up. I banged my elbow against the wall, but that was the least of my problems. I was away from the moonbeams. Now what?

Dad came into the room. He put his arms around me. "Bad dream, puddin'?"

"No, Daddy. I just can't stand all this moonlight."

"Moonlight?"

I nodded like the big baby I was.

"Hey, where's my Girl Warrior?"

Girl Warrior. I was nobody's super-shero. I buried my face in my father's chest.

"Daddy, can you move the dresser, then move my bed?"

"Why not just close the blinds?" he asked.

Mom had come into the room.

"Nightmare," he told her. "I got this."

Mom shook her head and went back to their room.

Paths to Discovery

"I had a close call," I whispered to Victoria, then glanced around. I didn't want to be overheard. "If I didn't move my bed from the gravitational pull of the moon, I'd be menstruating right now."

Victoria gave me her famous Queen Victoria look. The one that went with "Akilah, that is utterly ridiculous." She said nothing.

I took out my taunting essay. "Can you believe this? I couldn't even write free style. Mom said I had to stick to the facts." I would have said "empirical facts," but we hadn't done the word of the day since our last letter. It didn't make sense saying *empirical* if Victoria didn't spin it around with *spherical*.

"Oh! And then my mom handed me a gift. One she's been saving for the right moment. You'll never guess what."

Victoria *whatted* me with her eyes. Good enough.

"Kotex. *Kotex*. Can you believe that?"

Victoria hmmed.

"You couldn't have had a worse day in your life than

I had yesterday. The only way things could have gotten worse was if . . . if . . . ," but I stopped myself because I was launching into a joke and I wasn't supposed to do that. Make Victoria laugh.

I whipped out my permission slip and pointed to my mother's extra-large and extra-sharp signature. "Can't miss that. Geez." I put it back inside the folder. "Where's yours?"

She opened her notebook and showed me the yellow sheet. Nothing had been checked off or signed.

"Victoria! They're going to make you go to library science."

"Oh," she said, which was more than the hmm and the shrug.

I took out my pen and in my grownest *Mrs. Ojike*, I gave Victoria permission to participate in Paths to Discovery.

The following Monday Ida, Zuhair, Nahda, Sadia, and two other classmates whose parents checked the No box went to the library. If I hadn't signed Victoria's slip, she would have marched off with them. Ms. Saunders had Darryl roll the big TV out to the front of the room. She said, "I expect you to behave like the young ladies and gentlemen I know you are." Then she turned the lights off and pressed the Play button on the VCR.

Debra Wells had already told Victoria and me about it. First they show girls getting their period, then they show how boys' voices change and how their "thing" grows. They spend a lot of time on diseases, and they save the woman having a baby for last. They actually show it. The baby's head coming out and everything. Not that it's a big mystery. All you have to do is watch cable TV to see that. The only difference is, all through the video the narrator constantly says "you." Like those are your breasts budding and your hair growing in unmentionable places, only they mention it, and show it up on the screen. And you feel like they're pointing at you.

The music started before a picture appeared. It was nature music, all friendly and peaceful. The kind that plays while rivers flow and flowers bloom. Then the words *Paths to Discovery* popped up on the screen, and everyone was all eyes, leaning forward, waiting for something to happen. Something so shocking that six of our classmates couldn't watch it. Sure enough, the music got all high tech. Red and yellow molecules turned into a tadpole that turned into a fetus growing inside a woman's belly. Then, without warning, they showed a naked baby boy with his little dingdong, and all the girls laughed. I did too. I looked over at Victoria, but she didn't react. Next they showed a fat, pink baby girl with her legs open and you could see everything. The boys started to laugh.

Victoria got up while the naked baby girl was still on the TV screen. Just like that she was out the door. I stood, but Ms. Saunders told me to stay seated and went after her.

While Victoria and Ms. Saunders were gone, the baby girl and boy had stood up and transformed like teenage Autobots, sprouting hair under their arms and around their privates. The boy's "thing" and his "other stuff" grew big and just sort of hung there, and the girl needed a bra.

The class was going wild. Everyone was laughing like they had never seen anything like it. All you needed was for one object to be thrown and before you knew it, there was a full-scale paper war in Ms. Saunders's class. Crumpled snowballs flew left and right.

Ms. Saunders entered the room without Victoria and turned off the video. She flicked on the lights, *snap,* and told the class to put their heads down on their desks.

Victoria spent the rest of the afternoon in the library. At the end of the day, I wrote the homework assignment in Victoria's notebook and collected her books. I was trying to rush out, but Ms. Saunders stopped me.

She said, "When I learned that I would have both you and Victoria in my class, I was delighted. But now I am concerned."

I had to speak up for Victoria. I said, "I know Victoria's not working up to her full potential, but she really does belong in this class."

Ms. Saunders held up the yellow permission slip that I had signed. "Right now, Akilah, I am concerned about *your* potential."

I was in deep trouble. Tell-my-parents, call-the-principal type of trouble. My heart pounded like mad. You know, your life really does flash before your eyes at a moment like this. I saw myself cutting out paper dollies in the first grade and having a wee-wee accident in Pre-K.

"Frankly, Akilah, after speaking to Mrs. Ojike, I was

surprised to receive a signed permission slip."

My brain was stuck. I didn't know where to begin. All I could come up with was "I didn't want Victoria to go to library science."

"That is not an excuse, Akilah. What you did was quite serious."

When I took that sheet and signed it, I felt 100 percent right. Girl Warrior right. Why didn't anyone get it? I couldn't be separated from Victoria. Not again.

"Akilah. You're one of my brightest students. You and your classmates are growing up. That's why we're embarking on this new discovery," she said. "Your bodies are maturing, but your minds must always be ahead, and thinking positively. Now, young lady, I don't want you to continue in this way, so we will start anew, as if it's the first day of school and we are meeting for the first time. From this point on, you will be the person I know you are."

Vow

Victoria wasn't in the library. She was sitting out by the hopscotches like she did during recess.

"Here you are," I said as if I had just discovered her. In reality I stood and watched her for a while before I came out into the school yard. "I went to the library looking for you."

She didn't answer me, but I felt her willing me to sit next to her, so I did. We sat for a long time. Two or three minutes. Then she turned to me and said, "I don't look like that."

I didn't understand what she meant, but I knew she'd explain. As I sat waiting, a happiness ran through me. Like Christmas morning at six A.M. I was finally getting what I wanted. Today Victoria would return to me from wherever she had been.

Looking at me directly and not staring off, she said, "Akilah. What I am going to tell you is a secret."

We were already practically breath to breath, but I managed to move in closer.

"You cannot tell anyone."

"Okay," I said.

"Not *okay*," she said. "*Okay* isn't good enough. You must take a vow. Repeat after me: If I should tell, I will die."

I was stunned.

"Say it." She sounded like the real Victoria. I took her seriously.

"If I should tell, I will die."

"I will not tell my mother."

"I will not tell my mother."

"Even if she beats me."

"My mother wouldn't—"

"Say it."

"Even if she beats me." I laughed to myself. Auntie Cass wouldn't hesitate to draw her belt, but my mother would never, ever hit me.

"I will not tell a soul. Dead or alive."

I wanted to giggle when she said "dead." She raised her eyebrows. I repeated after her, "Dead or alive."

"Now show me your hands," she said. "I don't want you to cross your fingers."

I placed my hands on my lap where she could see them.

"Say I will not tell God, not even in my prayers."

My mother would have said, "God already knows," but I didn't dare. I said, "I will not tell God, not even in my prayers."

"Or I will die in Victoria's eyes, for she will no longer be my true friend."

I repeated all of it. A few minutes of silence passed before she said, "They showed the picture of the baby girl in class."

"Uh-huh."

"I don't look like that."

I didn't know what she meant. A chubby, white, baby girl with her legs open, showing her privates.

"Of course you don't look like her. I don't either." In fact, before Victoria left for Africa we compared our soft, fuzzy hair growing down below. Mine was more visible than hers.

"I don't have what girls have," she told me.

I still didn't know what she meant.

"They took it while I was sleeping."

"Took it?" She made no sense.

"My mother. My Auntie Omodara and Auntie Olefemi. My Grandmother Iyapo. They took me to see Doctor Ajala. I thought for more shots or to look at my teeth.

"First my mother inspected Doctor Ajala's knife, and then she told him to put me to sleep first. My aunties started yelling at my mother. They said things like, 'Do you think we will fail to hold her down?' My grandmother said she could have done it at home without so much fuss. She had done many girls, but my mother was very strong. 'We are modern,' she said. Then the doctor told everyone to be quiet. He could lose his license because it was illegal."

"Illegal?"

"Illegal. When he said *illegal*, my mind imagined the worst. I thought, How could my mother make us do something so horrible the doctor could lose his license? I could not imagine what it was. I was not sick. I did not need to see a doctor.

"But my aunties and grandmother would not stop yelling at her and at Doctor Ajala.

"My mother remained strong. She wouldn't give in to her sisters or her mother. She said things I was not accustomed to hearing her say. Do not ask me to repeat them."

She read my mind so well.

"Then the doctor put me to sleep."

"To sleep?"

"While he operated."

"Operated?" Now I sounded like Victoria had when she first returned. Repeating and questioning. My mind raced with horror and curiosity, and yet I made no pictures for what she was telling me. It was as though the picture-making part of my brain had shut down.

"When I woke up, I thought I was dead inside my body. I could see, but I could not move. Then feeling came back to me slowly, not on the inside, but outside of my body. Like I was a ghost, visiting Grandmother Iyapo's house. Sound around me did not seem real. I heard music, but it seemed far away, like echoes. I heard laughter and talking, but it didn't seem real.

"I still did not know what had happened to me. I did not remember coming back to Grandmother's house. I called for my mother. She helped me to the bathroom. I could barely stand. She had to hold me when I squatted. My ghost body fled, and my real body returned. When the pee came out of me, I screamed. I was being burned alive, but there were no flames creeping up my legs. For weeks and weeks I stood in a pot of fire."

"Fire?" I slowly began to feel, although I still couldn't picture anything. Only *knife, took, fire*.

She knew this and said, "Have you ever played Touch My Raisin?"

I nodded.

"And it felt good and tickly when you touched it?"

Only to Victoria could I admit this. "Umhm," I said.

"So good you didn't want to stop?"

I nodded again.

She pointed between her legs to what I call private place, the *Paths to Discovery* video calls genitals, and kids on the playground have nasty names for. She said, "When I was sleeping, they took my raisin."

My belly flopped. I felt dizzy. I didn't expect to hear what she told me.

"Mum said not to cry. All proper Nigerian girls have this done to stop the feeling."

"Stop the feeling?"

She said, "The feeling that comes from touching your raisin. I still cry."

"That's okay."

Victoria whispered, "When we returned home, you know, to Queens?"

I nodded.

"I locked myself in my room and got my mirror to squat over it and see. Akilah, after they took my raisin, they sewed my skin together to hide what they did."

Bam

I couldn't stand my father's voice calling me *puddin'* at the dinner table. The sweet stickiness of it turned the butter beans in my mouth sour. It made me sick, then angry, then mad.

"Can I be excused?"

I went up to my room, but I couldn't sleep. I couldn't stand the sheets against my skin. The pillowcase touching my head. The coils in the mattress. I couldn't stand my room. My brown-skinned, big-eyed dolls made me sick. The globe tilting upward made me sick. The books on my bookshelf, starting with *Nomusa and the New Magic*, made me sick. I read those books. I believed in them. My autographed soccer ball. My math and spelling trophies gleaming on the bookshelf. My stupid Girl Power flag. All made me sick. Sick. Sick. Sick. Girls don't have no power.

First I was angry at my mother for filling my head with stuff about Africa. Then I was angry at Dad for calling me puddin' and Girl Warrior. Then I was angry at Mrs. Ojike for taking Victoria to that illegal doctor. And angry at Mr. Ojike for doing nothing. I could see his big teeth smiling and hear him speaking politely while Victoria was screaming. But I was really angry at Nelson for telling me Victoria was getting over her illness. Liar. You can't get over what they did to her. You can't get over that.

Then I was mad. Crazy mad. Dizzy mad. Mad, mad, mad, mad, mad.

Tuesday Victoria and I walked to school together without saying a word. We sat at the hopscotches and stared out past the balls bouncing and the kids running and tagging each other and yelling.

In class we took our seats but did not volunteer to be class monitors or to bring the attendance sheets to the office. Victoria answered one question in math, one in science, and one in language arts. Not me. I couldn't raise my hand to call out a quotient, or share my knowledge about sharks, or identify one of the parts of speech. I couldn't talk about these silly things when anything could happen to a girl against her will. Against her knowledge. Against her body. Instead I did what Victoria did when she first came back. I let all the balls fly and the hands shoot up around us.

Once she told me, I felt like I was standing in the pot of fire with her. It didn't matter that her mother made the doctor put a needle in her arm so she would sleep while he cut her. And what if her aunts had held her down while her grandmother cut her body in their home?

I had to turn off my mind. I couldn't let my thoughts go flying off. I couldn't let myself imagine any more.

Wednesday Victoria and I were sitting by the hopscotches doing what we'd been doing for the past month. Except now we weren't just sitting in silence. We were making a statement. Depriving everyone of our girlness.

Jerilyn was looking for extra players for Ali Baba and the Forty Thieves. I wasn't in the hand-clapping, foot-stomping mood, so I shook my head no. Victoria did also. Jerilyn wouldn't take no for an answer. She had only five players, and she needed at least one more so everyone would have a partner.

"Just one game, just one, just one. Please?"

Her mother still does her hair.

"I said *no*."

"But y'all never play," Jerilyn wailed. "Y'all just sit there."

I felt so much older than Jerilyn. Older than every-body. All they had to worry about was finding another set of hands to clap Ali Baba and the Forty Thieves.

She gave up on us and went to Ida.

As soon as we got rid of Jerilyn, Juwan came over bouncing a basketball. I tried to stare past him, but he took up my view in his big, striped shirt. He knew we were ignoring him, but he kept bouncing his ball closer. So close the ball missed Victoria's foot by inches. She didn't react. Her hypnotic trick was amazing. Unfor-tunately I didn't have the art of ignoring knuckleheads down to a science. I reacted for her.

"Hey. Watch it."

"Or what?"

"You know what."

He stood there, threatening us, bouncing his ball. *Bam, bam, bam.*

"Speak, mummy, speak."

"Your mama's a mummy," I said.

He kept bouncing, but Victoria wouldn't give him any energy. That made him mad. *Bam.* He was too close, with his big stripes and big head. *Bam, bam, bam.* I could see the dust from the ball as it hit the ground. *Bam, bam, bam.*

"She went to deepest, darkest Africa and they turned her into a mummy." This time he missed her shoe by a centimeter.

"Shut up, you big fathead."

Then he started doing a stiff walk around us. We ignored him. That made him even madder.

"I bet if I hit her, she won't move. Know why? She's a mummy. A dummy mummy." Then he bounced the ball and it hit Victoria square on the toe of her shoe. *Bam!* I jumped up and hit Juwan as hard as I could in the gut. He hit me back, so I hauled back to China and let him have it, right on his nose. I got him good because my hand and his face were bloody. By this time kids swarmed around us, shouting, "Fight! Fight! Fight! Fight!" Then Mrs. Anderson, the recess aide, separated us. First we'd have to go to the nurse's office to clean up. After that, the vice principal's office. As we left the playground, I turned back to see if Victoria was all right, but Mrs. Anderson poked me and said, "March, young lady." The last I saw, Victoria hadn't moved from our spot.

Another Juwan Episode

While I was waiting for Miss Lady to pick me up,
Vice Principal Skinner called Mom at her job. All they
told her was there had been a fight and that she or Dad
had to come to school before I could return to class.
When they came home from work, Mom and Dad asked
if I was all right. I said yeah. But no one asked me what
happened, which was okay because I couldn't put it into
words. Not without justifying hitting Juwan, or betraying
my vow to Victoria.

Dad was mad. He didn't want to wait for the morning
meeting in Vice Principal Skinner's office. He had had
enough of Juwan Spenser's "fatherless antics" and
wanted to have a talk with Miss Spenser about her son.

"Where does that boy live?" he demanded.

"And accomplish what, Roy?" my mother said.
"Where do you think the bad seed sprang from?"

"That boy needs to learn how to treat a young lady."

Mom sighed heavily. She was more tired of Dad than
upset about the whole Juwan thing. "We'll handle it at
school, Roy. That's why we received the phone call. To

iron it out with a school official. That's the right thing to do, and we do what's right."

She had been through this too many times to get excited. In Pre-K Juwan spilled a carton of green paint all over my picture because mine looked better than his. In the first grade he smashed my hard-boiled Easter egg for no reason. Each year, except for the third grade, there was always an incident between Juwan and me.

Dad finally gave in. "You're sure you're okay, puddin'?"

"I'm okay."

"That's my Girl Warrior. Brave and beautiful. Show me that left hook."

"Roy."

I wasn't sure what would happen in Vice Principal Skinner's office the next morning. As far as my parents were concerned, this fight was just another Juwan episode. During those parent meetings in the vice principal's office, Mom spoke calmly and politely to Miss Spenser. But underneath her calm was an attitude that said, "I don't expect anything more from your child." Mom is sort of a snob. She always points out other kids' public behavior—mostly black kids—and says, "There's no reason for you to behave like that." That's why she likes the Ojikes, besides their being from Africa. She thinks the Ojikes are quiet, refined people. Mom describes Mrs. Ojike as Queen Nefertiti herself. Graceful and regal. Victoria giggled when I told her. Victoria said,

"Doesn't your mother know that Queen Nefertiti was Egyptian? And dead?"

I giggled, hearing Victoria's voice in my head. Then I realized, I wasn't the only one nervous about tomorrow. Victoria was probably worried about what I'd say to justify my socking Juwan. Victoria knew that my talking is like my essay writing: once I get going, I can't stop myself.

I had to let her know that I wouldn't break my vow, no matter what. I got on-line before I went to bed and sent an e-mail to QueenV3: "If I should tell, I will die."

That Thursday morning we were all standing in the hallway outside the principal's office. Miss Spenser and Juwan. Mom and me. Mom told Dad to go to work. There was no need for all of us to gang up on Miss Spenser.

After awkward greetings between our mothers and a long silence in the hallway, Juwan's mother said, "I suppose you think *my* child started it."

Mom was sure Juwan had thrown the first punch. So sure she didn't even ask for my side. Mom just said, "We shouldn't have this discussion in the hallway."

Then Vice Principal Skinner, a tall, light-skinned man with wavy, combed-back hair, opened the door and welcomed us in like he was hosting a PTA meeting. Vice Principal Skinner wore a gray suit with a burgundy tie. Come to think of it, Vice Principal Skinner always wore a suit. He attended a lot of parent meetings.

Juwan told his side first. He said, "I was dribbling a

basketball, not even bothering them, and she punched me in the nose."

My mother wasn't an eyeball roller, but this time she couldn't help herself.

Miss Spenser said, "I don't send my son to school to fight. Your child"— she pointed at Mom—"should keep her hands to herself."

Mom coughed to keep from laughing. If I didn't know my mother was going to punish me later, I would have truly enjoyed all of this.

Vice Principal Skinner said, with the utmost confidence in me, "Akilah, tell us your side."

I stood up, cleared my throat, and said, "I hit Juwan Spenser as hard as I could." Then I took my seat.

Sitting with Miss Lady

You do not apologize when you are not sorry.
You do not pretend that you've learned your lesson even if you are allowed back into class by saying those two little words. Even if Vice Principal Skinner promises to take your reasons into account. Even if your mother orders you to apologize and is humiliated and angry when you will not. Even if Miss Spenser uses your refusal to apologize as a weapon against you and your mother. Even if you will face an unimaginable punishment when you get home. You do not apologize when you know that you would do it again.

My mother was furious. Too furious to speak to me as we walked home.

"Go upstairs," she said. "Don't come out for any reason whatsoever." She sounded like Auntie Cass telling my cousins, "Go get me a tree switch."

I was called downstairs for dinner later.

I could bear my mother's anger because it made me brave, like a warrior going through a trial. That was how

I felt fighting for Victoria. Like the true Girl Warrior my dad always says I am.

What I couldn't take was my father's disappointment. His woundedness. His face.

"Why, Akilah? Why?"

"I can't talk about it," I said.

"Why?" he persisted. "You don't have to be afraid of Juwan."

His babying me made Mom fly into a rage. "She better be afraid of *me*! She better be afraid of what *I* might do!"

I was sent to my room to reflect.

The doorbell rang. I peeked out of my window and saw the top of Victoria's head. She had brought my books and homework and probably my classwork for today and tomorrow. That's what your "class buddy" does when you are sick. Nelson stood at her side.

I wanted to love Nelson once again and feel myself falling over a cliff at the sight of him. I kept myself steady, remembering that Nelson didn't stand tall when Victoria needed him. Only *I* was prepared to do that.

I watched Victoria and Nelson walk past the elm trees and out of view.

For the next three school days I had to stay with Miss Lady while my mother went to work. Miss Lady seemed pleased to have something to do besides walking Gigi and picking bugs off her rosebush. She sat on a stool and watched as I converted decimals into fractions. She watched as I read two chapters of *Last Summer with Maizon*. Then she watched as I wrote my book report.

"None of that staring into space, young lady," she said whenever I paused to collect my thoughts.

"I have to think before I write," I explained. This is true, because my mother goes through my reports and essays and writes, "What do you mean by this?" whenever she thinks I'm talking out of my head.

"No dawdling, Akilah. I want your mother to see your progress."

Mom made it clear that I was not to enjoy myself in Miss Lady's home. There was to be no TV, no radio, no long talks about nothing, and no playing with Gigi. Obviously Mom knows nothing about Gigi. That fussy little pom-pom doesn't like kids and doesn't play with anyone.

At noon Miss Lady made lunch for us. Tuna salad with mustard, no mayo. She said mayo was too oily and unsettling. She gave me an apple instead of cookies or chips. Miss Lady said young people were too fat and full of junk. That made me laugh, the way she said it. Full of junk.

Miss Lady is slender. Never had any kids. At least I didn't see any pictures anywhere, only framed ones of her and Gigi. Right then I decided that twenty years from now, I'd forgive Nelson and marry him. I didn't want to have a house filled with only dog pictures.

I got started on science, my last subject. All I had to

do was read a chapter, but Miss Lady didn't believe me.

"Then tell me about these"—she squinted to get a better look—"sharks."

Miss Lady followed along as I told her about the evolution of sharks over 400 million years. When she was satisfied that I had been studying and not making stuff up, she said, "That's good. Continue reading."

I was glad she didn't quiz me afterward. My eyes might have been following the words in the chapter, but my mind was on Victoria. I was missing her. Our silences together. Her shoulder next to mine as we sit in the school yard. Then I missed Ms. Saunders, and school activities, and recess. I missed the lunchroom smell on pizza days. The unmarked surface of my desk. The intercom announcements in the morning. Working with stencils in art. Learning a new song from Kenya.

When you start to miss people and things from the depths of your soul, you can taste, see, and feel every good thing you're missing. You don't recall the bad parts. That is for sure. After three days of sitting in Miss Lady's house, reading and writing and eating mustard tuna sandwiches, I didn't have one thought of Juwan. Not one. Even the details of Victoria's horrible operation started to cloud up in my mind.

I understood why people are sent to prison. It's so they will miss everything good around them and regret what they did to be incarcerated. That would have made a good word of the day for Victoria and me. *Incarcerated.* I was tired of being incarcerated.

By my last day of being away from school and cut off from my privileges, I didn't feel like a warrior standing tall for Victoria.

I wanted to play video games with my dad.

I wanted to sit up under my mom while she scratched my scalp and braided my hair. We hadn't done that since I was nine and declared myself old enough to do my own hair.

I wanted to be with my 5–2 classmates, raising my hand like a maniac.

I wanted to get back into my world.

The doorbell chimed at a quarter of six. For the last time Mom had come to collect me. Before we left, she opened my loose-leaf binder while Miss Lady reported my activities and confirmed that I hadn't enjoyed myself one bit.

I said thank you and good-bye to Miss Lady. Gigi was glad to see me go. She jumped and barked, showing more excitement than she had during the entire three days of my incarceration. Mom also thanked Miss Lady and gave her money, which Miss Lady said was not necessary. Then we walked down to our house in silence.

I washed up, made the salad, and set the table. Then Mom, Dad, and I sat down, said the blessing, and passed the food. For the fifth and final time Mom asked, "Are you ready to explain yourself, Akilah?"

For the fifth and final time I told my parents, "No. I am not."

Honored

"I hope you've used this time out productively,"
Vice Principal Skinner said. Today he wore his blue suit.

"Oh, she has," my mother spoke up. I felt a little sorry for Mom. It was hard for her, suddenly being the mother of the bad kid.

Mr. Skinner was also sympathetic toward her. "I don't doubt you, Mrs. Hunter," he said. His eyes were kind.

To me he was stern. "Akilah, we do not solve problems with our fists," he said. "Violence is never a solution."

A framed portrait of Dr. Martin Luther King Jr. hung on Mr. Skinner's wall, just above his head. You couldn't look at Vice Principal Skinner sitting behind his desk without seeing Dr. King.

While Mr. Skinner talked about problem solving, I thought, Maybe I wouldn't have punched Juwan if I hadn't known what they did to Victoria in that doctor's office. Maybe I could have outsmarted Juwan, or told Mrs. Anderson on him.

The fact was, I knew what had happened to Victoria

and I was mad. Sick, angry, and mad. I *told* Juwan not to mess with her, but he wouldn't stop. He just kept on and kept on until he hit her. Then I stepped up to defend her. I had to. No one else would.

Suddenly I felt stronger. Not broken down, like when I sat in Miss Lady's house. I knew why I hit Juwan and why I wouldn't apologize.

"Say something, Akilah," my mother urged. She was still humiliated and embarrassed that Miss Spenser had outmothered her.

"Can I return to my class now?"

Everything looked the same when I entered the classroom and took my place next to Victoria. Juwan snickered at me, but I couldn't care less. Only Ms. Saunders's opinion bothered me. I was glad to be back in class, but I could barely face her. If I did, I would have seen the betrayal and disappointment in her eyes, even behind her glasses.

Ms. Saunders and I were supposed to be starting over on a clean slate, but I had gone back on our deal. I was not the Akilah she knew I could be. I was a bad kid who got suspended for fighting.

Still, I was determined to keep my vow to Victoria. I wouldn't try to explain myself. Not even to get on Ms. Saunders's good side.

Victoria and I found our usual spot during recess. Jerilyn came over as soon as we sat down.

"I hope you know I can't play with you anymore," she said to me. "Because you've been suspended."

Jerilyn had pink teddy bears in her scrunchie. She waited for a response, but I wouldn't give her one. She left us alone.

"Did you get my e-mail?"

Victoria nodded.

"I didn't tell them," I said.

"I know."

"How are you sure?" I asked.

Victoria looked me over from head to toe, then said, "I thought you might tell if your mother beat you. But I see you have no welts or bruises on your legs."

"My mother'd never beat me. And even if she did, I still wouldn't tell."

"I'm glad," she said. "I thought you might start to tell a little, then tell everything."

"I know," I said. "But I didn't. I kept my lips zipped. And I won't apologize, either."

"I know."

We had four more minutes before recess ended. Victoria didn't say another word while we sat out by the hopscotches, but she didn't have to. I replayed her saying "I'm glad" and "I know" in my head like songs. Besides those one-word answers she gave in class, I was the only person she really talked to. I was honored.

Ayodele

I was still on punishment, although Dad had long ago caved in. I felt sorry for him. He had no one to play with, so he raised our basketball hoop up to NBA height because it was about time I learned to shoot a proper jumper.

Nothing had changed as far as Mom was concerned. She was determined to teach me a lesson. I knew she felt betrayed after all of our backyard tea talks. When we were down in Silver Spring, she bragged to her sisters about how we talked openly about everything. In reply Auntie Cass said, "Mark my words, Baby. That will soon change."

In spite of being on punishment, I didn't miss TV like I thought I would. Besides, everyone talked about what was on TV in the lunchroom the next day. It was doing stuff on my computer that I missed. I could use my computer, but "for educational purposes only." Mom made herself perfectly clear. While I was up in my room, there was to be no playing music, no endless surfing, and no computer games. "No amusement whatsoever" were her exact words.

She didn't want to hear any laughter, period. She was still mad that I wouldn't talk or apologize. As always, Dad tried to jolly me at the dinner table that evening. Mom gave him a look.

My homework was done. Plus the extra-credit work. Everything checked and rechecked. My school clothes were ready for the next day. My backpack was loaded. I had two hours before bedtime. Two whole hours, with nothing to do but stare at the paint on the walls. How many times could I read the same books on my bookshelf? I was going to die of boredom.

I wanted to talk to Victoria, but even if I could call her on the phone, I'd have to do all the talking. I'd slip in something funny to make sure she was listening on the other end. And then she'd hang up on me.

It wasn't fair that we couldn't laugh together. I mean, I understood why she didn't laugh out loud, but we should be able to laugh, just between us.

Then I realized I had a purpose for being on the computer. Mom said I could use my PC for educational purposes, and finally I had one. My search wouldn't involve laughter or amusement of any kind.

I powered up my computer and turned down the sound controls so I couldn't be heard. Instantly I was out on the web. All I had to do was search, but for what? Girls with no laughter? It wasn't like looking up menstruation, where all you need is a topic and correct spelling. I didn't have a name to start with.

I thought hard. What they did to Victoria was cruel,

so I typed in *cruelty*. That was too broad. I tried *extreme cruelty* and got links to animal rights articles, stuff about the death penalty, and a heavy metal band. Then I said to myself, "Akilah, use all the clues. Use what you know," so I typed in *cruelty to girls in Africa*. It took a couple of seconds for the search engine to pull everything together, but *ka-bang!*—236 sites found. I was in the right place.

At first all I saw were links to circumcision web sites, but that couldn't be right. Circumcision is for baby boys. There's nothing to circumcise on a girl. We don't have extra skin covering our privates. We just have what we have. But then the next link said, "Female circumcision."

Female circumcision?

Then another link said, "Female genital mutilation, another term for Female circumcision." I knew *genital*, from the backyard tea talks and from *Paths to Discovery*, but *mutilation* gave me trouble. It had to be a form of mutation and mutant. You read enough comic books, you know about mutants. Things that change. I right clicked on the word *mutilation*. "Maim, disfigure, destroy."

That was what they did to Victoria. They mutilated her.

That sick feeling came over me. I wanted to understand, but I didn't want to know. I was stalling. Scrolling to see which site I would enter.

One said, "FGM practiced in the United States." I couldn't believe it. It wasn't just in Africa. It was here, too. And in other countries. But no one was talking about it. It wasn't in the newspapers or on the evening news.

I was running out of hiding places. I couldn't believe

there were so many sites. If I was going to learn more, I had to enter.

Then one link caught my eye, probably because the summary began with quotation marks. A real person talking. I clicked on it. I read aloud, but in a whisper:

"I am nine. My name is Ayodele. *Ayodele* means 'joy.' I do not have joy. I do not laugh. I do not run and play like my little sisters, Ife and Aya. Soon they will not have joy either."

There were quotations from other girls. Some younger than I am. Some older. I couldn't believe it. All of these true stories. Most of them written by another person who told a girl's story for her.

I could do this, I thought. I could go into these sites and find out why. I could tell Victoria that she wasn't the only girl that it happened to. There were hundreds of girls. No, thousands. No, millions!

I clicked on the site that began, "Over two million girls mutilated each year." There was also a warning about graphic pictures on the site.

I wasn't afraid. I could enter for Victoria.

"AKILAH!"

I froze.

Mom stood in the doorway. She was mad. "Which part of 'No amusement whatsoever' do you not understand?"

Behind me was the screen. A black background with large, white letters flashing, "Over two million girls mutilated each year. Caution: The following pages include graphic material."

I couldn't move. I just stood there, hoping my body blocked the screen.

"You are out of control, young lady. I am yanking this thing out of here now."

She moved me aside and went for the power switch, but then she stopped in front of the screen. She made a sound. Not a scream, but like a cry. Like how I felt inside when Victoria first told me what they did to her.

She grabbed my hand. "Why are you here? In this site?"

I couldn't speak. Then I started to gather myself, and *couldn't speak* turned to *wouldn't speak*. I swallowed my spit.

"Why are you here?"

Not even my lips moved.

"Akilah, tell me now. Why are you looking at this web site?"

Not if my mother beats me. Not even to God in my prayers.

She exhaled and put her hands on her face, I think to cool down. She sat on my bed and said, "Sit here with me."

I obeyed, but I didn't make a sound.

"Akilah. Remember our talks in the backyard? You know that you can tell me anything."

This was the part where I was supposed to say, "I know," but I didn't answer.

"Does this have anything to do with Victoria?"

My eyes must have jumped or shifted in a way that only she could read.

"You can tell me," she said softly, even when I felt her struggling to keep from screaming.

I wouldn't budge. Anything I would say was as good as telling.

If I should tell, then I will die.

My mother left my room.

Like a Rocket

Mom paced and circled and shook her head.

Dad hovered over her and kept asking, "What is it, Gladys? What's wrong?" Every step he took toward her, Mom turned away. It was like a dance.

Finally Mom threw up her hands and said, "I can't, Roy. I just can't talk right now. Akilah and I have to go."

"It's almost eight," he said. "Where are you going? I should go with you."

"No," she said.

"If this is about Juwan—"

"Roy, please," Mom said. She turned to me and said, "Akilah, tie those laces. We have to go. Now."

She took me by the hand and we left. She was muttering to herself in between telling me to keep up.

I tried to walk faster, but I didn't want to. I should have gone to the bathroom first. My stomach cramped into a thousand knots, and my head was throbbing. I tried to tell her I didn't feel so well, but she was like a rocket headed straight for the Ojikes' house.

One thing was certain: My mother knew what female

genital mutilation was and that they had mutilated Victoria.

I could barely walk. My bones were turning to Jell-O, my stomach was cramping, and I kept thinking that Victoria would soon hate me.

There was nothing I could do to stop my mother. Mom was set to take child-saving action, like removing Victoria from the Ojikes' house, or telling the police, or reporting the Ojikes to Child Welfare, where she worked. Then Mr. and Mrs. Ojike would be arrested. Victoria and Nelson would be deported to Nigeria to live with their grandmother—the same grandmother who had mutilated many girls. Or instead of being deported, Victoria would be put in a group home. That was part of my mother's job. Rescuing kids from bad homes and putting them in group homes or in foster care.

Or maybe Mom would tell the newspapers and TV stations about Victoria's mutilation. Cameras everywhere would flash and click at Victoria like she was a criminal or someone to feel sorry for. Then everyone at school would point at her and whisper. Or they'd just come out and ask her what it felt like.

I counted backward in my head, wishing us back. Back inside our house. Back before mutilation. Before I knew what it was and before it happened to Victoria. Just back. All Victoria had ever asked me to do was keep a vow and to not make her laugh.

"Mom," I moaned, "let's go home."

It was too late. Mom rang the doorbell and Mrs. Ojike

welcomed us inside with a warm smile. Before she could finish offering us tea or *fufu*, Mom came out and said, "Is it true? Did you have Victoria circumcised?"

Mrs. Ojike didn't expect that. She was stunned.

Mom asked again. Clearer. Louder. "Did you have Victoria circumcised?"

By this time, Mr. Ojike had entered the living room, but no one else had followed him. Still, I could feel Victoria behind the walls. She had to know that I was on the other side with my mother.

Mrs. Ojike told Mom, "That is a private matter."

Mom said, "That is barbaric. Inhumane. How could you do this to your daughter? Your very own daughter?"

Mrs. Ojike said, "You are American. These are not your customs. I do not expect you to understand."

Her words *You are American* seemed to wound my mother, although Mom tried to hide it. She was steeling herself, after being told she was not at all African.

"That may very well be true," my mother said. "But there is nothing you can say to justify the savage ritual of mutilating your child."

At that moment Mrs. Ojike became the queen my mother always described. Even with her back against the wall, she was unruffled and dignified. It was as if Mrs. Ojike looked at Mom the way my mom looked at Juwan's mother and thought, I expect this from you. No less. No more.

Mrs. Ojike told us, "You are not welcome here. Leave my home."

The porch light went off as we stepped outside. When I looked up at their house, all of the rooms went black.

My mother reached for my hand, but I held it back. "Look what you did!" I screamed at her. "You caused trouble!"

My mother grabbed my hand, but I yanked it away. Then she raised her hand like she was going to smack me, but she stopped herself and pointed at me instead.

"Akilah, do not ever take that tone with me as long as you live."

I knew she wasn't playing with me, but I wasn't playing with her, either. I didn't care what happened to me. With Victoria gone, I didn't have anything left to lose.

"I gave Victoria my word I wouldn't tell."

"Akilah, you can't be silent about a thing like this. You should have told me," she said. "When something is wrong, you make it right."

"You didn't make it right," I said back. "You made it worse."

She walked ahead and told me to keep up.

I refused to walk by her side. I didn't care how dark it was, or that the only light came from the street lamps and the three-quarter moon. I was burning mad. So mad that I didn't care about the sudden warm splurt in my panties. I didn't care that the moon had finally tagged me.

A Little

I knew what to do when I came home. I stood on my desk chair and reached for the sack of sanitary napkins in the back of my closet. Instead of soaking my panties in cold water like *she* had told me to do, I balled them up along with my stained jeans and stuck them in my bottom drawer.

I didn't want anything from her. Not any Tylenol, or blackberry tea, or long talks. If I never heard her voice again, it would be too soon.

Except that I couldn't escape her. She was hysterical. I could hear her telling Dad about Mrs. Ojike and what they had done to Victoria. It was like she was waving a flag. Her own discovery. Her next rescue mission.

Mom hadn't thought for one minute about Victoria or the danger she had put her in. She had gone flying over there like a rocket, accusing Mrs. Ojike of being barbaric and inhumane. What if the Ojikes punished Victoria for telling? What if they packed up and moved in the middle of the night? Had Mom considered that? Had she?

I was never going to see Victoria again. I knew it. At

this moment Victoria must be calling me a liar, I thought. A big, fat, ugly liar whose vow meant nothing. At this moment Victoria must think she is alone and has no one to trust. At this moment Victoria must hate me.

The next day I sat by the hopscotches alone, then sat next to an empty desk in class. When I got home, I rode my bike up and down her block with that stupid napkin squished between my legs. It was like wearing a diaper. Being a ten-year-old woman sucked raw eggs.

I kept riding from one end of the block to the other. Back and forth. Back and forth. No one came outside, but the curtains moved once. I sat on my bike and waited, but they didn't move again. I finally rode home, at least satisfied the Ojikes hadn't packed up and fled to Africa.

I stayed away from my mother because I didn't want her to notice that I was menstruating. She made me sick. I answered her "yes" and "no," and I showed her my homework. But that was all she could have from me. The bare minimum. Like Victoria's one-word answers.

I went through my routine at school without Victoria. It is hard to make a statement alone, because no one knows you are making one. Sitting next to Victoria in silence made me feel strong. Sitting by myself just made me feel alone.

I approached Ms. Saunders at the end of the day and asked, "Do you know when Victoria is coming back?"

Ms. Saunders said she could not discuss one student with another. Then she dropped her face to finish writing in her teacher's notebook. It was more polite than saying, "Go away and don't ask any more questions." I pretended I didn't get it.

"Well, can I bring Victoria's homework and math quiz to her? I'm her class buddy." We had gotten our math quizzes back. Both Victoria and I scored a ten out of ten. I had seen her paper before she handed it in. We had the same answers.

"That won't be necessary," Ms. Saunders said, "but thank you, Akilah." She tried to smile, but then quickly went back to writing in her notebook, face down.

Ms. Saunders knew something.

I walked past the buses and vans lined up along the curb. Juwan stuck his head out the window of a big, cheese bus. He rolled a piece of paper—probably his quiz—into a ball and then threw it at me. He missed. I didn't even feel like singing, "Ha-ha." I just tossed my head and kept walking.

Later I rode my bike to Victoria's house, hoping she'd come outside. It would take me two seconds to say, "I kept my vow," before Mrs. Ojike chased me away with a broom. I pictured that clearly: Mrs. Ojike chasing me with a broom.

As I rode in semicircles, waiting for either Victoria to come out or to be chased away by her mother, I saw Miss Lady walking Gigi toward me. She said, holding a little bag of dog poop, "If the girl's mother wanted her to come outside and play, she'd be out here."

I felt like saying, "Shut up, Miss Lady," but Miss Lady

would tell my mother in nothing flat. Then I'd never see daylight again. Not that it mattered.

I rode my bike home. I didn't have any homework. Ms. Saunders had given me a homework pass as a reward for scoring a ten on the quiz and getting an Excellent Perspective on my *Maizon* book report. Since I had nothing better to do, I went on-line. Mom never did remove the computer from my room. She just said to be careful where I surfed, and that she knew how to check which web sites I visited and the files I downloaded. I didn't care, as long as I could go on-line.

I logged on and started looking for new computer games. Then *pop*! I had an instant message.

QUEENV3: Why?
GIRLWAR: I didn't tell her.
QUEENV3: Liar!!!
GIRLWAR: I swear I didn't.
QUEENV3: LIAR!!!
GIRLWAR: She saw when I was on-line.
No message.
GIRLWAR: I found the web site. I know what they call it.
No message.
GIRLWAR: Circumcision
No message.
GIRLWAR: And mutilation
No message.
GIRLWAR: Mom saw the web site b4 I cd ESC.
QUEENV3: YOU TOLD HER.

GIRLWAR: She figured it out by looking.

No message for a long time.

QUEENV3: My mother wants to put me in the International School.

GIRLWAR: She can't!

QUEENV3: They have no openings. She will try again next semester.

GIRLWAR: I'm glad.

QUEENV3: You can't come to my house. Ever.

GIRLWAR: I know.

No message for a long time.

GIRLWAR: I got my period. I'm bleeding.

QUEENV3: I don't have my period yet. I'm bleeding too. A little.

The Subject Was Victoria

The week slipped by without sight of Victoria.
I sent her e-mails, but no one answered. I surfed around, hoping she'd feel my presence on the Internet, but there were no more instant messages from QueenV3.

I got on my bike and rode around napkin-free for the first time in five days. I was so glad my period was over. Not that it was horrible. It was just there, like having a wad of gum stuck to the bottom of your shoe. You can't take a step without knowing it's there, but when you scrape it off, you're finally tip-tapping along like nobody's business. It doesn't seem right that boys don't go through anything remotely like a period. They should go through something.

I was on my way home from the park when I saw Nelson jogging ahead. He was in his blue and gold warm-up suit. I sped up until I was practically on him. He turned around.

"You're on my heels," he said.

"I know," I replied.

He was annoyed, but I didn't care. He slowed his

pace, but I still had to pedal to keep up. He stopped running.

"What do you want, Akilah?"

"I want to know why you didn't protect Victoria. She's your sister."

"You do not understand." He wouldn't look me in the face. He started to jog again. He was running away.

I wouldn't let him go so easily. I called after him, "I understand, all right. You let them mutilate your sister while you did nothing."

Nelson stopped and faced me. Maybe he was embarrassed that I could holler something like that out in the street. "Akilah, these are not your customs. You cannot understand these matters."

"'Cause there's no real reason for what you all did to her. That's why you can't explain it."

I knew Nelson himself had not taken Victoria to that doctor, but he and his father were just as guilty as his mother, grandmother, and aunts. If his aunts had held Victoria down while his grandmother mutilated her at home, he would have sat in the other room with Mr. Ojike, discussing rugby.

Nelson didn't have an answer and started walking away from me. I didn't let that stop me from following him. I was going to ride his shadow until he came up with something better than "These are not your customs."

"You will not leave me alone," he said.

"Nope," I answered. "Not until you explain."

I didn't anticipate him stopping so suddenly. I

couldn't hit the brakes in time and rammed into him. He hobbled, then dusted himself off. I didn't care that he was glaring at me. I wanted my explanation.

"So?"

He sighed, blowing a heavy breath on me. I used to live to be this close to Nelson. To feel his breath on me no matter what it smelled like.

"How do I make you understand, Akilah?"

"Easy," I said. "Tell me something that makes sense."

He just stood there looking over my head to avoid my eyes.

"Men do not talk of these things, Akilah. This is women's business."

He didn't look so manly.

"Victoria couldn't tell me why. All she knows is what your mother said. That Nigerian girls get it done to stop the good feeling. You know, from touching yourself. I mean, it's not like girls have their hands down there touching themselves all the time like boys."

Nelson was mortified, but I didn't care. Why should I be ashamed? You're only ashamed if you're guilty, and I didn't have anything to feel guilty about.

"It's done to keep the girl . . ."

"From being a nasty girl," I completed.

"Akilah, when I marry, the girl will be a clean and proper Nigerian girl. She will not be, as you put it, a nasty girl."

He was making me mad. "Clean and proper?"

"Yes, Akilah. For marriage, a woman must be clean.

Proper. Untouched by anyone."

"And how will you know that?"

"I will know by the way her parents present her to my family and me. Her mother will tell my mother that she is a proper Nigerian girl and that she has been prepared for marriage, to become a wife."

"You mean all cut up and mutilated." He was confusing things, talking about getting married. The subject was Victoria and mutilation.

"I don't know why I tried to explain this to you, Akilah. You are American. And a child."

A few weeks ago that would have hurt, Nelson calling me a child. Now I didn't care how he saw me.

"Victoria isn't trying to be somebody's wife. She's a girl. Your sister."

He sighed again. I wished he had bad breath so I could really not like him, but he didn't.

"One day you will want to marry," he told me. "If you were from my village, your future husband's family would not welcome you into their home if you have been ruined."

I told him, "You ruin girls when you mutilate them. You ruined Victoria."

He turned to leave, but this time I let him go. I didn't even follow him with my eyes. I pushed off on my bike and rode down the street toward my house.

Rite of Passage

School wasn't the same without Victoria. I answered questions when asked and handed in my homework on time, but my mind wasn't really on spelling tests, projects, and reports. One afternoon I got halfway home from school before I realized I didn't have my science book. My book bag was too light. I ran all the way to the school and banged on the door, hoping the custodian would hear me. Finally Mrs. Jenkins, a hall aide, opened the front door.

"School's over, young lady," she said. "You're headed the wrong way."

"My science book is upstairs," I said. "I can't do my homework without it." I was still out of breath.

Mrs. Jenkins didn't want to let me inside. Hall aides can't leave until all of the students are out of the building.

"Fifth grader?" she asked.

"Yeah," I said. "Ms. Saunders's class."

"Well, be quick. I don't want to come upstairs looking for you."

I ran up the steps to the top floor, hoping to find Ms.

Saunders gone and the classroom door unlocked. No such luck. Ms. Saunders was in the hallway, fixing something in the display case.

"Akilah," she said. "You've ruined my surprise."

In the center of the display, between the Halloween masks we made in art, were two large, wooden African masks.

"I wanted to surprise you all in the morning."

"Sorry," I said. "I forgot my science book." I went inside and got it. When I came back out, Ms. Saunders was still adjusting one of the masks, which wouldn't hang straight.

"They're ceremonial masks," she said. "A gift from my Kenyan students."

"Oh."

"What, Akilah? No facts about Kenya or ceremonial masks?"

She was teasing me, but I wasn't in a teasing, Encyclopedia Brown mood.

"We have a lot of African stuff at home," I said. "I'm not much into Africa, anyway."

A set of footsteps came clacking down the hall. I turned around. It was Mrs. Jenkins.

"It's all right," Ms. Saunders called out to her. "I'll escort Akilah out of the building."

Mrs. Jenkins waved to Ms. Saunders, then left.

Ms. Saunders locked the display case and stood before it, admiring the masks. She wanted me to like the Kenyan masks the way my mom wanted me to like my African dolls.

"Since when are you 'not much into Africa,' Akilah?" She was still teasing me. She said it with a smile.

"You outgrow stuff," I said.

"So suddenly, Akilah?"

I shrugged. "Ms. Saunders, Africa isn't everything you've read about. Tomorrow everyone will see those masks and think they're great. Then you'll tell us about the mahogany trees they came from and how the masks were carved with knives. But I'll bet you won't tell us how they carve girls with those knives."

Ms. Saunders's smile thinned. She said, "Come inside," then closed the door behind us. She pulled Ida's chair up next to her desk, and we sat down.

"I did more than read about Africa. I taught in Kenya for four years."

"I know," I said.

"It was a rewarding experience, Akilah. But it also challenged me.

"Teaching school there was nothing like teaching school here. I had students of all ages in my class, and often they were absent. It was hard to keep lessons going, but I managed. Anyway, I started to notice my seven-year-old girls were disappearing, one by one. When I asked the headmaster—he is like the principal—he was reluctant to answer me. Exhausted by my inquiries, he finally said, 'It is a private matter. None of our concern.'"

A private matter. That was what Mrs. Ojike told my mother before she made us leave her house.

"Still," Ms. Saunders continued, "I wanted to learn about the culture. I asked everyone about the disappearing girls, but no one would talk to me. Finally, the woman who washed the desks and floors took me aside and explained what they did to little girls."

"Mutilation," I said.

"Yes," Ms. Saunders said. "I couldn't believe it was true. But then I noticed how the older girls walked, with a careful glide."

Shlush, shlush, I thought. "Like Victoria."

Ms. Saunders nodded. I knew she couldn't discuss one student with another, so I spoke.

"Victoria told me what they did to her, after she ran out of that class. You know. Paths to Discovery."

"Ah," Ms. Saunders said. That brought back memories for both of us. She and I were supposed to have begun with a clean slate after that class. Ms. Saunders said, "I started the semester with one silent student. And then I had two."

"I couldn't talk about it, Ms. Saunders. I made a vow to Victoria."

"You were protecting your friend," she said. "Even if it meant risking punishment. These eyes see a lot, Akilah. They could always see the real you."

I was glad of that.

"Neither one of us knew what to call the thing they had done to her. I kept searching the web until I found the words."

"Female circumcision," she said.

"And female genital mutilation."

"That is a lot for a girl to know."

"It's a lot for a girl to go through," I said back. "It's wrong."

"It's not part of your world, Akilah. I myself couldn't understand it at first, but I tried. It was one of my many challenges. To understand."

"I'll never understand," I said. "Victoria's mother said it was to stop the good feeling."

Ms. Saunders said, "That's part of it."

"Her brother said mutilation makes girls clean and proper. A girl can't get married unless she has that done. The groom's family wouldn't want her."

Ms. Saunders nodded. "The practice of mutilation is tied to marriages. I've been to several weddings in Kenya. The families negotiate for a long time before a wedding can take place. Believe me, there is nothing to negotiate if the girl has been sexually active, if she is no longer a virgin. Akilah, you remember when we talked about the dangers of sexual activity?"

"Yeah," I said. Thanks to that class, instead of getting tagged with cooties out on the playground, you get tagged with STD, a sexually transmitted disease.

"You can't bring anyone unclean into a new family. A young woman who has not been circumcised is not considered clean, or a woman, for that matter."

Clean and proper, I thought.

"It's not right, Ms. Saunders. You're a woman because that's what you are. Not because someone mutilates you."

Ms. Saunders squinted and gave me a weary smile.

She said, "I'm not going to argue with you, Akilah, but I'm challenging you to keep an open mind. If Victoria had lived in her family's village all of her life, she might have been prepared for her rite of passage."

"Never," I said.

I knew what she was trying to do. She wanted me to see the other side. I refused to let my mind bend in any direction where mutilating girls was okay.

"Ms. Saunders, you don't even know the real Victoria like I do," I said. "She doesn't want to get married. She wants to rule a country." That sounded silly, but that was her plan. To follow her heroine, Queen Victoria, and rule a country.

"Mrs. Ojike is transferring Victoria to another school," I added.

"We'll see," Ms. Saunders said.

I didn't think there was anything to see. Victoria hadn't been to school for a week. Even though the International School had no openings, I doubted whether she was coming back to our school.

Ms. Saunders glanced at the closed door, then said, "Thanks to your mother, Victoria is getting some help—but that is all I can say."

I got excited about the possibilities for a moment. "Can she be put back?" I asked. "Can they make her the way she was?"

Ms. Saunders said, "I think we can help Victoria to accept what has happened. But no one can make her the way she was."

It's about Time

If I were walking home with Victoria, I would
have said, "*Ambivalent*. The word of the day is *ambivalent*."

You know how you have words stored in your head
because you've heard them or read them, but you've
never had a reason to use them? Well, I could have used
this one: "Ambivalent. I feel ambivalent toward my
mother."

How could I forget that she burst into my room and
stole the secret between Victoria and me? A secret I gave
my most solemn vow and risked punishment to protect.

Without thinking about the consequences, she went
charging over to Victoria's house and got Victoria in trouble with her parents. Then got me in trouble with
Victoria. And on top of it, she wouldn't admit that she
was wrong.

And while I was mad at her, and waiting for her to
admit she was wrong or at least apologize, Mom was getting help for Victoria.

Ambivalent. The word of the day is *ambivalent*.

• • •

From the end of our block, I could see my father stuffing orange garbage bags with elm leaves that had fallen into the front yard. Last year I begged him to buy those orange garbage bags with the jack-o'-lantern faces so our house would be the only one on the block with them on Halloween. Now I was embarrassed to watch my father stuffing and shaking those giant plastic jack-o'-lanterns.

Practically every window on our block was decorated with pumpkins, witches, and skeletons. I was ten years old and hadn't even thought about my Halloween costume. Usually by now Mom and Dad would be arguing about "the appropriate costume" for me: Cleopatra, Bessie Coleman, or a basketball-playing ninja. I always ended up making my own costume.

"What are you supposed to be?" Victoria asked the first time we went trick-or-treating together.

I put together a box, mop head, and a hula hoop. I said, "I am a Game Boy." I was eight.

There was no mistaking who Victoria was. She only went as the queen of England. One year she wore a tiara. The next year, a pillbox hat. She always wore white gloves, carried a scepter, and was made up with pink lipstick over false buck teeth. She was regal.

This year I'd probably stay home and hand out candy to the little kids. That would please my mother. She doesn't like knocking on our neighbors' doors begging for candy, then inspecting every wrapper in my loot bag. She throws out half of my candy anyway.

Dad, on the other hand, loves Halloween and any

other chance to do this kid stuff with me. He says he can't remember a single one of his own Halloweens, Christmases, or birthdays. I think he does remember them. He just doesn't want to talk about them.

Satisfied with the shape of his two garbage bag pumpkins, he placed one on each side of the porch.

"Hey, puddin'."

"Hey, Dad."

"How's school?" he asked.

"Okay."

"No trouble from you-know-who?"

"Dad."

"Just checking."

"You know about Victoria, don't you?"

He nodded.

"No one's supposed to know," I told him. "But *she* went running over there, pointing and accusing."

"Whoa, whoa, whoa, little girl. *She*?" He meant the disrespectful way I referred to my mother. He sat down on the porch steps. I sat next to him.

"Mom caused trouble for everyone," I said.

"Your mother may have reacted emotionally, but in the end, she did all of the right things. Victoria is going to get some help, you know."

"What kind of help?"

Dad just said, "Help."

Ms. Saunders knew. My dad knew. Everyone knew what was going on but me.

"You mean a shrink?"

"Psychologist."

I mimicked him. "Psychologist."

"You are like your mother."

I gave the "am not" look, but that only made him chuckle. My dad is really handsome, especially when he laughs like that.

"Akilah, if you knew what would happen to Victoria before she left for Nigeria, what would you have done?"

"Stopped them."

"Your mother's exact words."

Of course I didn't want to hear that. I was still feeling ambivalent.

"If something is wrong, we right it. That's who we are. That's what we do. We don't stay silent."

Those were her words too.

"So, uh, puddin', don't you have something to tell your mother?"

"Like what?" I asked.

If Dad wasn't so brown, he'd have been purple. He looked embarrassed, but I couldn't figure out why. Then he made a face like he had smelled something rancid. Now, if I were truly like my mother, I would have said, "Spit it out, Roy." I just sat there without a clue, watching my dad turn colors.

"You might want to tell your mother, uh, that, uh, you, uh, had your first . . ."

"You know?" I was mortified.

He nodded. "Did your mother, uh, also tell you about, uh, proper disposal?"

I hid my face in my book bag.

"What am I going to do with two women driving me crazy?"

"I'm not a woman," I said. "I'm a girl."

I went up to my room. As soon as I opened the door, the funk hit me. I guess you can't have that stuff lying around.

I took the ruined underwear and the jeans that I had stuffed in my drawer and put them in my laundry bag to bring downstairs. I gathered up my collection of sanitary napkins, each one folded and taped into tight Easter eggs.

Mom was sitting in a lawn chair reading a book when I came out back. Next to her on the patio table were two mugs and a thermos. I went over to the garbage can and dumped the sack of napkins. When I clanked the lid over the garbage can, she put her book down and said, "It's about time."

The Twenty-first Right

"You know, girl," Mom began.

"What, girl?" I replied.

"You did well. You didn't panic. That's the main thing."

I sat in the other lounge chair and waited for her to finish. She poured green tea from the thermos into our mugs.

I steeled myself, expecting Mom to scold me about hiding my period or for stinking up my room. She just sipped, smiled, and stared off over our fence.

Once I knew it was safe, I told Mom, "I was prepared."

She surprised me. She hadn't called my aunts to tell them the news. She hadn't cooked a special dinner to celebrate. There were no green tea libations raised up to Mother Moon and no mumbo-jumbo speeches about my journey into womanhood. There wasn't even a first period story. I guess we had already done that.

People say females are better at talking things out. We also know how to share silence.

The warm mug felt good in my hands. I inhaled the

steam. Me and Mom. Sitting in the backyard sipping tea, coasting back into normal. I didn't give yes-no answers and she didn't act like a madwoman.

Well, I knew my mother wasn't a madwoman. She just did what she thought was right. Maybe because what happened to Victoria was so wrong. When I thought about it, everyone believed they were right. The Ojikes, Victoria's grandmother, her aunties, and Ms. Saunders. Everyone. But no one asked Victoria. She didn't have any rights. She didn't have a say. She was still silent. Not like Mom and me enjoying the evening fall air, but locked silent from not knowing why they did that to her.

All of a sudden I couldn't enjoy being outside with my mom anymore. I was mad because everyone was right and Victoria was silent. Well, Victoria had spoken to me, but we still couldn't laugh together. And that wasn't right.

The word *right* kept singing in my head. *Right, right, right.* Like lyrics to a song I couldn't shake. But by the twenty-first *right*, I heard something I hadn't heard all those times before. By the twenty-first *right*, I heard the answer to Victoria's silence. Or at least, a start.

I asked if I could be excused to go on-line. Mom was still staring off and said, "Yes, Akilah. Feel free."

I ran up to my room and powered up my computer. It's a start, I thought. But what would Victoria think? It couldn't work without her.

I made my e-mail short and coded, in case she had to read it quickly. I typed, "When something is wrong, we write it."

You Must Be Proud

I was playing Ali Baba and the Forty Thieves
with Jerilyn, Janetta, Ida, Nahda, and Sadia. Jerilyn was
my partner. She kept messing up, clapping on three-four
and flip-flapping on five and six, instead of stomping.
Meanwhile I managed to keep up, even with my mind
elsewhere. It's amazing how sometimes when you con-
centrate so hard you mess up, but when you free your
mind you're clapping, stomping, and flip-flapping without missing a beat.

Jerilyn messed up again. She was in the middle of
one of those "sorries" when I looked up and saw Mrs.
Ojike at the gate with Victoria. My heart leaped. I was so
glad to see Victoria, I left the rest of the hand-clappers
hanging in the middle of Ali Baba and went running to
the gate. I wondered if she had logged on and read my e-
mail. We had lots to talk about.

Mrs. Ojike called out, "Victoria!"

Victoria said, "I cannot associate with you," and
turned her back to me.

I didn't want to get Victoria into any more trouble, so

I ran back to the hand-clappers.

Mrs. Ojike didn't move. Even when it was time to line up, Mrs. Ojike stood at the gate and watched us, to make sure Victoria and I didn't line up together.

I marched at the end of the girls' line and thought, Mrs. Ojike couldn't watch us in class, but I was wrong. I entered our classroom only to discover Ida had been moved to Victoria's desk, and Victoria was up front near Ms. Saunders. Mrs. Ojike had thought of everything.

Cafeteria seats weren't assigned, I thought. At lunchtime I grabbed my tray and sat next to Victoria.

"You cannot talk to me," Victoria said.

"I'm not talking," I said. "I'm eating."

We ate our lunches without speaking to each other. I wanted to prove to her that I would not get her into trouble. I was still her friend.

While I was controlling the urge to talk to Victoria, something hit me in the back. A Milk Dud flew over my shoulder and into my string beans. I turned around and found a skee-ball-faced Juwan grinning at me. He was sitting between Richie and Darryl, who tried to look like they didn't know anything about flying Milk Duds.

I knew what Juwan was after. He was trying to make me lose my mind, but I wouldn't fall for it. I turned around and kept eating.

"Akilah," Janetta urged. "You gonna take that?"

He threw another Milk Dud. This time he aimed at Victoria. She kept eating her ravioli, but I stood up. I could see myself giving a war cry and leaping over the lunch table like a ninja. Instead I went over to the lunch-room aide and said, "Mrs. Hall, those boys are throwing Milk Duds at Victoria and me."

Mrs. Hall was only too happy to come over and straighten this out. Adults love to remind you that kids are starving all around the world while you are playing with food. It didn't matter that the "food" was Milk Duds.

Seeing how mad Mrs. Hall was, both Richie and Darryl ratted Juwan out. "He did it," they both said, pointing at Juwan.

"Not me," Juwan said in his most wrongly accused voice. "I wasn't doing nothing." He was even more con-vincing than when he made his speech in the vice princi-pal's office.

"Did so," Richie said.

"I told you, man," Darryl said. "Just step to Akilah and say, 'Akilah, I like the way you raise your hand in class.'"

"I do not like her!" Juwan protested.

Darryl said to Mrs. Hall, "Juwan said, 'Watch this. I'm gonna make Akilah turn around.' Then he started throw-ing those Milk Duds at her."

The whole lunchroom went crazy laughing. They were laughing more at Darryl's imitation than at Juwan. Darryl could be a real clown. Mrs. Hall wasn't laughing. She was marching Juwan to the vice princi-pal's office.

All the girls at my table, especially Janetta, thought it was funny. She wouldn't let me finish my string beans in peace. When lunch was over, we lined up and followed Ms. Saunders back to our classroom. Before we entered and took our seats, Victoria tapped me and said, "Juwan Spenser. You must be proud."

American Troublemaker's Daughter

I expected Victoria to be long gone by now, but there she was, sitting at our spot near the hopscotches. The last of the school buses was pulling off.

I was so excited to see her and wanted to know if she got my e-mail. Before I sat down, I asked, "Can I sit here?"

She looked at me and said, "Can you?"

I wanted to be sure it was safe. That I wouldn't get her into trouble. "Where is your mother?"

"She couldn't come. She told Nelson to walk me, but he does not want to be bothered. Mum will be cross to know that he has left me alone with the American Troublemaker's Daughter."

Those were our new names to the Ojikes. My mother was American Troublemaker and I was American Troublemaker's Daughter.

"Your mother knows many people," Victoria said. "And they know people at the consulate where my father works."

I knew it. Mom went to Mr. Ojike's job with an army of Child Welfare workers.

"Is that why you speak to a shrink?"

"I do not speak. The shrink does all of the speaking. But no writing. She uses a tape recorder."

I wanted to laugh. Victoria's voice was so funny, like an English African robot's. The real Victoria's voice.

"Why don't you talk to her?"

Victoria said, "I am helping her to become a better shrink. At night she can play her tape and hear her voice assuring me it is okay to speak. That is what she wants me to do. Speak."

"But she will help you," I told her.

"She will shrink me."

I hit her on the arm. Not a hard hit. A play hit. I hadn't done that since we were fourth graders. "They could put you in a psychiatric bin."

"It is either the loony bin or psychiatric ward," she corrected. "Do not mix them up."

She sounded like herself. All she needed was her Halloween scepter.

I remembered when we first met at the monkey bars. I felt like she was calling me an intelligent hyena.

"You should talk to the shrink," I told her.

"I should not."

"They'll split us up next year. They'll put you in the special class for kids with problems."

"If I'm still here," she said. "My mother put me on the waiting list for the International School. She keeps trying to transfer me, but there is no space and the waiting list is long."

Her eyes twinkled, like ha-ha.

"Well, you should at least speak to the shrink."

"I will speak to the shrink and to others when it doesn't hurt."

"Girl, are you crazy? That may be never."

She lifted her head, and said, "Do you know who I was named for? I was named for Queen Victoria. She, who ruled nearly half of the world. She, who commanded the largest fleets in all the seas. If the queen wishes not to speak, the queen will not be made to speak."

You know how you start out serious and then it falls apart, and the only thing you are is ridiculous? Well, that was how Queen Victoria looked at that moment. Bulldog proud and ridiculous. I knew it and she knew it. She giggled. And I giggled. We giggled a lot. It felt good.

"So why are you sitting here?" I asked.

"I am waiting."

"Waiting?"

"To hear your plan. What will we write?"

I was excited. Ecstatic. I said, "We can write a letter. Like the girl on the Internet—Ayodele."

"*Ayodele* means 'joy,'" she reminded me. "Sometimes you are renamed. I am sure Ayodele has a new name by now."

I had a naming ceremony when I was born. My parents videotaped it. My dad lifted me up in the air and they named me Akilah, while my aunties, uncles, and cousins looked on. Auntie Cass whispered something to Auntie Jackie about "mumbo-jumbo nonsense." It is all on the videotape.

I understood why Ayodele might want to change her name, but me change my name from Akilah? "Intelligence"? Nah.

"What will we do with this letter?" Victoria asked.

"We will put it on the web, for the world. We can warn girls everywhere."

"Girls everywhere with computers," Victoria said.

Hmm. I hadn't thought of that.

"Well, we have to start somewhere," I said. "Everyone gets to say why they're right. You should tell them why they're wrong."

Victoria thought about it for a while. She said, "We must use good words in the letter. Like *atrocity*."

"*Monstrous*," I chimed in.

"*Criminal*."

"*Extreme cruelty*."

"*Inhumane. Barbaric. Savage ritual*," she said.

"Those are my mom's words."

"Your mother uses good words."

We shared a long silence. Just us. Victoria and Akilah. Then it was time to go. If we didn't leave now, her mother or brother would come looking for her. I didn't want to live up to my new name. American Troublemaker's Daughter. Not when we had a new secret to protect.

We walked and plotted best ways to part before we neared her block. She would go first, then I would let two minutes pass. As soon as she was inside her house, I'd walk down, on Miss Lady's side of the street.

Before we split up, Victoria said, "Do not tell the others that I can laugh. I do not want them to think that it is okay."

I said, "Okay," and let her walk ahead.

Author's Note

Years ago I dragged my daughters, Michelle and Stephanie, to a friend's baby shower. I was amazed by how quickly Stephanie, who was eight, bonded with my friend's daughter, Asha, also eight. They giggled as if they'd known each other for years. I thought, We should all be eight-year-olds, laughing as freely as we pleased. No sooner had I said this to myself than my mind jumped to eight-year-old girls who didn't laugh so freely. It occurred to me that eight is the age at which many girls in some African countries undergo the brutal ritual of female genital mutilation (FGM). Within moments, as I watched the two girls sharing whispers, giggles, and then laughter, I knew I would write this story.

Every year approximately two million girls undergo FGM. In spite of laws to ban this custom, FGM is still practiced in at least twenty-three African countries. Immigrants have brought this custom to the United States, Canada, and Europe. (During the nineteenth century, FGM was also performed by European doctors to cure what they believed was female hysteria, but this practice was later abandoned.)

FGM is typically performed under nonsterile conditions by persons without medical training. The dangers faced by girls and young women who undergo FGM include permanent damage to sexual and reproductive organs, psychological trauma, infection, hemorrhaging, and death.

Because the tradition of female genital mutilation has been embedded into these cultures for hundreds of years, it remains a struggle to end its practice. In spite of the struggle, human rights activists continue to educate the world at large about the plight of girls and young women in countries where FGM is practiced, as well as provide support for those who have undergone the ritual. In addition to fighting for more laws to enforce a ban on FGM, human rights activists also encourage practicing cultures to adopt gender identification and rite of passage alternatives. In fact, in a ceremony in Koroso Village in Guinea, a small country in West Africa, more than one hundred women surrendered their knives used to perform FGM on girls.*

Although FGM is performed on young girls, materials written for young readers about this topic are scarce. Readers seeking information about children around the world and their coming-of-age customs should visit their community libraries and bookstores. You may also write to me about *No Laughter Here* at ritawg@aol.com.

*"A Voice for the Eradication of Female Genital Mutilation," *Awaken 4*, no. 1 (April 2000): 13.